Eagles Talon

Bears and Eagles Three

R. P. Wollbaum

First Published in Canada by Midar and Associates Ltd.
2015

Copyright © R.P. Wollbaum 2015

While some of the events and characters are based on historical incidents and figures, this novel is entirely a work of fiction.

ISBN: 9780994024954

All rights reserved. No part of this publication may be reproduced, stored in a retrieval system, or transmitted, in any form or by any means, electric, mechanical, photocopying, recording or otherwise, without the prior permission of the publisher.

Table of Contents

Chapter One...6
Chapter Two..48
Chapter Three..66
Chapter Four...93
Chapter Five..111
Chapter Six...124
Chapter Seven...147
Chapter Eight...186
Chapter Nine..211
Chapter Ten...249
Authors Notes...271

Chapter One

May 1918

John ducked out of his tent then stretched kinks out of his back and took the coffee his aide handed him. While the brigade had been ready in two weeks, it had taken another two months for the government to arrange transport for them to the seaport in Vancouver. Another month was spent waiting for shipping and, once embarked, it had taken two months to arrive in Cairo, where they had waited in a temporary camp for a week before being assigned a billet in the main area.

During that time, the Canadian Army had taken part in a large number of successful operations in Europe, earning itself a reputation for its innovation and ferocity in battle. That the Regiment had not been involved was grating on the members of the brigade – the troops were itching to get into the action. The few veterans of the African conflict just shook their heads and kept quiet. The youngsters would find out soon enough.

Another week they had spent sitting around waiting for instructions. A week of putting up with comments from the ANZAC and British contingent about the best light cavalry outfit in North America sitting on their hands for three years while the rest of them were out fighting. Requests for meetings with the British command had gone unanswered and John was beginning to think the war would be over before they contributed at all.

The regiment had no number or name. They just called themselves The Regiment. But the other Allied troops started calling them the Eagles Bears and Beavers for the animals depicted on the regimental flag, and then shortened that to the EBB.

Today he was summoned to a meeting with high command – God willing it would be deployment orders. As the brigade now numbered four thousand troopers, John had been promoted to Brigadier General against his wishes. He was in fact the troopers' recognized leader and a mere colonel would not be in keeping to command a group as large as this. In order to forestall any attempt by the British or Canadian armies to appoint a general officer to command the group, the Eagles had promoted John.

His aide handed him his jacket and field officer's cap and, along with the four other members of his senior staff, John marched into the command office, where he was ushered into a large briefing room.

In the room were already assembled an Australian and two British generals along with their staffs and a curious-looking major wearing a British major's uniform with an Arab head covering. After an initial look over, the rest of the room ignored the Canadians, making no effort to make introductions or introduce themselves.

"Is it me, or is it as frosty in here as a blizzard out on the prairie?" John said, laying his hand on one of his aide's shoulders to stop him making a rude reply to a jibe from one of the ANZAC junior officers, who while being admonished by his commander drew laughs from the rest of the group.

"They have been in the thick of it for years while we were sitting on our asses back home," he whispered into the aide's ear. "They have every right, so keep quiet until you have also earned that right."

Any further comment was cut off by the entrance of the commanding general into the room and the order to take their seats was given. Adding further insult was the fact that there were no seats for the Canadians. John motioned his men to join him against the back wall, where he took position facing the podium, leaning against the wall with his arms crossed on his chest. His men took similar positions to each side of him.

"Gentlemen," began the commander. "The Tsar in

Russia has abdicated his throne and the country is dissolving into anarchy and revolution. We expect the Russians to withdraw from the Eastern Front and can expect the Huns to relocate the majority of their forces back to the Western Front shortly. It is therefore of the utmost import that we put pressure on the Turks and push them hard, to force them out of the war and free up manpower for what we assume will be a major thrust from the Germans this spring in France.

"We have been joined by the EBBs to assist us in this matter. I had the pleasure of serving alongside this brigade in Africa and I can tell you that if the current troops are half as good as their fathers were, they are welcome indeed. In fact, they have been petitioning their government since the beginning of the war to come to this theatre of operations and it took a direct intervention from the King himself before the Canadian government would allow them to come. Then the government dragged its feet in getting them here.

"They are the best equipped and trained force in the Commonwealth today, gentlemen. They have been training all of the best troops the Canadians have in France. In short, I believe they are the best of the best. General Bekenbaum there was commanding a squadron in Africa that took part in the wildest and fiercest battle of the whole campaign: with minimal losses to themselves the Eagles defeated a force four times their size in less than two hours."

The general paused at this point as the rest of the room looked back at the Canadians.

"What is it your brother said at the end, John? What did you expect, they were only farmers? Farmers, gentlemen, who had beaten the very best that Britain had sent at them, myself included. So no more talk of shirking duties, eh? Now down to business."

A large map of Palestine on the wall was revealed, with lines marking the enemy positions and areas to be attacked. Each battalion was assigned one of the areas and the Canadians were still waiting to be tasked when the general had finished assigning all of the blue arrows to the various Commonwealth commanders. Again looks were thrown their way as the rest of the room became aware that the Canadians would be once again sitting this one out. That was when the strangely dressed major approached the podium and with a pencil began drawing another series of blue lines and arrows around the sides and to the rear of the enemies' red lines. He explained that the smaller lines would be the Arab forces striking at the rear, while the larger blue arrow on the eastern side of the attack plan symbolized the EBB.

"Gentlemen, you are to be the demonstration attack,"

said the general to the ANZAC and British commanders. "The Turks are expecting you, know you are here and are waiting for you. The EBB is fully mechanized and has its own artillery, and will hit them hard where they cannot possibly defend. In short, gentlemen, the EBB better be as good as they say or they will get their arses handed to them. They will be on their own behind the lines, and we will not be able to relieve them. General Bekenbaum, you will coordinate with Major Lawrence here – and please have your wireless operators coordinate with our men. Timing will be everything, gentlemen. Good day."

As the group began to leave the hall, once again ignoring the Canadians, Lawrence introduced himself to John.

"They treat me the same way, sir," Lawrence said. "You get used to it after a while."

"Situation normal for us, Major," said John, leading Lawrence back toward the Canadians' camp. "We are used to being snubbed. By the Brits, or the Russians and even the Germans. We have a job to do; we are not here to make friends."

"How soon can you be ready to move, sir?" asked Lawrence. "We have fifty miles to travel to get to our jumping-off point."

"An hour too late for you, Major?" answered John.

"OK, boys, get the lads ready to move. Get the frequencies from the Brits and get the rocks out of their pants," John ordered and their camp quickly disintegrated into organized confusion, as tents were dismantled and trucks loaded.

Each vehicle, in addition to tents for its crew, had two days' worth of food and water for each crew member. Every vehicle had a least one Lewis gun mounted on it. The transport trucks had them mounted on pedestals behind the co-driver. Spring-clip mounts on the dashes held the transport drivers' rifles ready, and every trooper had a Colt automatic pistol.

The rear wheels of each vehicle were dueled – they had two drive sets instead of one as on the civilian models. A heavy sprocket was attached to the outside leading rear wheels and another on the front steering wheels. If the vehicle became bogged down in mud or snow, a heavy chain would be attached to the sprockets, enabling all the wheels to power the vehicle. A set of tracks was also available to fit around the rear wheel sets if required.

This drive set up had been developed after several years of testing in the mud and snow at home base. In expectation of being sent to hot and dry areas, tests had also been conducted on a Canadian government military reserve five hours to the east of home base, and two of each vehicle type had been sent by train to the deserts of Arizona. Overseen by American army observers, the vehicles had been put through rigorous trials and returned home to be torn apart to look for faults.

    The light-duty scout cars were based on the Ford Model T. Rolling chassis had been obtained, and their frames elongated and stiffened up. Heavier axles and springs were added and axel ratios changed. Instead of light sheet metal and canvas bodies, these were made of steel plate. The engine and radiator cover were angled instead of vertical, as was the windscreen. Louvers could close to protect both in the event of an attack. The armor had been tested and would stop a .45-caliber bullet fired from ten meters. The scout cars had transmitters and receivers installed, which took up most of the room in the vehicles. Crews were made up of a driver, co-driver/gunner and radio operator/gunner. Four of the scouts would leave ten minutes before the rest of the brigade and fan out across the intended route: their purpose was to seek out enemy positions first, then any problems with the route that would have to be dealt with.

    The rest of the vehicles used a frame obtained from Autocar and engines and transmissions from Cadillac.

Autocar provided the two-speed drive axels, and other components were ordered from other after-market suppliers and assembled at a General Motors of Canada plant in Ontario before being shipped to Didsbury by rail, where weapons and radio systems were installed. DND (Department of National Defense), had expressed an interest in the designs and the regiment had granted a license to GM of Canada to use the designs for sale to other governments for ten percent of profits.

    The next to leave were six armored cars. Each of these had a moveable enclosed turret mounting a Vickers machine gun; they were heavily armored and enclosed, with gun ports located along the sides and rear of the vehicle. Each of them had radio equipment and a Lewis Gun that could be mounted on a ring around a hatch at the rear of the car or fired from the inside through the ports. Each crew member also had a rifle and pistol. Their purpose was to go to the aid of scout cars and hold and engage enemy until the rest of the brigade could engage.

    Preceded by another six armored cars came the troop transports. These had armored fronts, sides and rears; the tops were open but could be canvased covered. Here too a Vickers machine gun was centrally fixed on a ring mount and Lewis guns were mounted on opposing front and rear corners. Each of the transports held ten Eagle troopers. These troopers would dismount from the vehicle to form assault teams, taking one Lewis gun with them. Three Bear troopers were in the cab: one driver/radio operator, one co-driver/gunner and one radio operator/gunner. They would stay with the vehicle once the Eagles had dismounted.

    Next came vehicles of the mortar section, followed by vehicles towing the first battery of field guns. After that came the vehicles hauling spare parts, food and ammunition, as well as ambulances and medical equipment transport and the all important fuel trucks. The command radio vehicles were in the center of this group. Then transport trucks again followed by the second battery of field guns, the other mortar section, the other half of the Eagles, six armored cars to the rear, and another four scout cars. Six more armored cars were spaced, three to a side, along the side of the column.

    Within an hour, all the vehicles were moving, spaced several meters apart. This not only cut down on the amount of dust the vehicle occupants had to contend with, but ensured that no more than one vehicle would be hit by incoming artillery rounds.

Five hours later they crept into their assigned position under cover of darkness.

"Make camp," John ordered. "Cold camp: we are in the middle of Indian country."

"As rough as that truck ride was, it was better than horseback," said Lawrence, walking up to John. "We could have stopped at night fall – we don't attack for two days time."

"Didn't want to alert the enemy with a dust plume," responded John, observing his men take only bedrolls down from the trucks and breaking into cans of rations for their supper. "How close are we?" he asked.

"They are in a valley on the other side of this hill, about two miles away," answered Lawrence. "We can probably see their campfires from the summit."

John waved his artillery and infantry commanders over to him and gestured for Lawrence to lead the way. It was cloudless and there was a full moon, and they had little trouble negotiating their way up the small hill. True enough, the enemy camp was in view below them.

There was little chance of the enemy seeing them as the moon was in front, leaving the observers in the dark. Even so, they all crouched down to minimize their profiles in case anyone should happen to look their way. They could tell from the number, positioning and the size of the cooking fires that the camp was large and about a mile away. Little else could be determined in the low light, even using binoculars.

"They seldom send out patrols at night," said Lawrence. "The Arabs have a habit of ambushing them and killing them all. If they come out at all, they will come out in a large force."

"OK," John said. "Have sentries posted on this hill and at dawn I want us up here scoping out that camp."

John was up well before dawn, and he and his commanders, with several subordinates each, were climbing the hill and were in position lying across the top with binoculars to their eyes as the sun began to warm their backs. The camp was laid out along a valley with a river behind it. The tents were positioned neatly and apparently by company and battalion order. Horse lines were well away from the camp and two batteries of field guns were positioned to the rear. There were two distinct groups. The larger held three battalions of infantry and two squadrons of cavalry. The smaller was a single battalion and one squadron of cavalry.

"Well, well," John said, after glassing the flags positioned in the two camps. "We have a few Huns here. That should make things a bit more interesting."

The reverse slope of the hill was steeper than the one

they had just climbed, but would pose no problems. John began mapping out areas of concern in the camp and any terrain features that might cause the vehicles problems. After about an hour they crawled back down to a place where they could stand unseen from the camp below, then walked back to their own camp.

"Breakfast time," ordered John. "The wind is with us, so small fires. First priority is the commander's coffee."

"Here, sir," said Ralf, his batman, a veteran from Africa. "Breakfast for the gentlemen will be up shortly. The men will be eating before you are, sir. These petrol stoves work very well in the field."

John nodded his thanks then turned to his artillery colonel. "George, I will want those batteries eliminated first," he told him. "Then the machine-gun emplacements. Then you can concentrate on any strong points we uncover."

"No problem, John," replied George. George Von Hoaelde was his father's friend Rudy's grandson, and had risen through the ranks to command the vital large ordnance. "Our batteries can engage theirs while the mortars get working on the machine-gun nests."

"Fine," responded John. "Ed, I want the armored cars in the forefront buttoned up. You will lead the way and have the infantry behind in support. I want five cars to circle behind and contain. Each of those cars takes ten troopers. We want to cut them off from retreating in that direction. Make sure they are heavy with Lewis guns, and Ralf, assign some support to them in case they need it."

"No problem," said Ed.

"Everyone get on separate frequencies and I want one radio from each squadron tuned to my frequency. Radio silence until we go over the top, understood?" John ordered.

Receiving affirmative answers, he dismissed his commanders to make their own preparations for the attack the next day.

"I say," said Lawrence. "You fellows don't waste much time now, do you?"

"What's there to plan? The camp is there, we are here, we go there," answered John.

"You did more planning in an hour than most of the Brits do in two days," Lawrence said. "They would be signaling Allenby right now asking for instructions and possibly RAF over flights to confirm their suspicions."

"In a lot of situations that would be correct procedure," said John. "We, however, will be attacking a couple of hours after the main advance begins. The enemy will be reacting to that, so we won't have to worry about unexpected troop movements. Those Turks and Germans do not know we are here and they are not expecting us. After we hit them: that is when the situation will change. Do we exploit the situation or not? I will call Allenby then for clarification. Not before."

"I would like to take the credit, Major," said John, "but these are standard Cossack tactics my family has been using for generations. Most of my troopers would make the same plan in this situation as I would. The only difference between me and my forefathers is we have updated equipment and weapons. The tactics are the same. Hit them hard and fast from an unexpected direction. If it doesn't work, we fall back, regroup and try again in another spot."

The rest of the day, John was in full view of his men, sitting under an awning stretched over the top of his command vehicle. Lawrence observed this remarkable leader and his remarkable men as they made their unhurried preparations for the upcoming operation. Occasionally a messenger would arrive reporting completion of some task, or asking direction and advice for another, but for the most part, he and John had the place to themselves.

John had noticed that Arab tribesmen were appearing in small troops on horseback, Lee–Enfield's across their backs, each group making themselves known to Lawrence before they camped on the fringes of the camp, observing the Canadians from a respectful distance.

"They will be joining us tomorrow," said Lawrence. "It is their country after all and they feel they must have a presence."

"Understood," John replied. "Just let them know to stay away from our fields of fire. I don't want to be killing any Allies. We will be hitting the enemy from here, but it would be nice if they could get some of their cavalry on the other side of the river to grab anyone trying to escape that way. I would also like them to discourage any of the enemy from escaping to the south."

"I will tell them in the morning," said Lawrence. "Some of these tribesman think more of money than of country, so best they don't know our plans – then they can't tell the Turks anything no matter what they're offered. By the time I tell them, it will be too late to warn the camp."

Lawrence began to notice a strange behavior among the Canadians. The men, some in small groups and some individually, would walk by the command post and gently stroke a standard propped up against the truck holding the command radios. After each man touched the standard's worn casing he would look at John and nod, and receive a nod back from John in return. These Canadians are very odd he thought. The troopers, men and women, began to quietly take down their rifles, cleaning and oiling already clean weapons, making sure each part functioned properly, before lovingly putting them back under cover, but close to hand. All except the old timers, who walked about in their old style campaign hats, Mauser rifles slung on their backs.

"Those men are veterans from our fight in Africa," said John, nodding toward the old timers who came as a group to the standard, drew to attention, saluted it, did the sign of the cross then one by one walked by, John nodding at each of them.

"They are more comfortable with the weapons and gear they survived that fight with," John continued. "They will most likely switch the Mausers out for Enfield's after."

"Is their significance to the ritual they're all performing?" asked Lawrence.

"Yes," was the only answer he received, and he knew better than to push for more.

The grey dawn saw the arrival of a full squadron of well-mounted and -armed Arabs. The other Arabs and Lawrence approached this group, Lawrence saluting their leader and addressing him before escorting him to John. Today, John was wearing his old campaign hat with a maple-leaf badge pinned to it, his 1911 Colt automatic strapped to a shoulder holster and a bandoleer containing pouches of .303 stripper clips across his shoulders.

After introducing the Arab leader to John, Lawrence explained that the Arabs would observe the attack at first, then join in wherever they could find a weak spot, not encroaching on the main attack. John thanked the man, who spoke excellent English, turning down the offer of coffee, explaining he had to brief his men, and left.

All talk and movement in the camp stopped. The horizon lit up in bright flashes, followed shortly by the loud distant thunder of guns – it was the beginning of the demonstration to the south. The gunners took this as their cue to take position, break out ammunition and set up their preliminary sight adjustments. The infantry gathered their equipment and stowed away anything but gear required for the assault, while the armored car personnel checked over the vehicles and readied the Lewis guns mounted to them, two to a vehicle. Now the old timers took down their beloved Mausers, checking them, and made sure everything was in readiness, rounds ready to hand and loose in pouches, knives and Colt pistols ready for use if needed.

As the sun rose the camp settled down until only whispered conversation among the troops could be heard and that seldom. All eyes on John and the command truck.

"Fall them in, Sergeant Major," John ordered quietly, rising to his feet and placing his old campaign hat at the Jaunty Cossack angle.

Quickly and quietly the brigade formed up into their troops and squadrons, all ranged before John, who was now standing on the lowered tailgate of his truck. Lawrence was standing on the ground beside John's aide, who had a notebook in his hand and was writing down everything that was happening. Then John began to speak, not in English, but in Russian, and Lawrence looked over the aide's shoulder: he was writing down what John was saying in English.

"Comrades, it has come time to pay back for all the privileges and good life the motherland has provided us. It is time to help another people throw off the yoke of oppression of the Turk and to be allowed to experience freedom as we ourselves have done. This is the price of freedom. We must help others who are oppressed. Canada has been good to us and our families and now Canada is asking us to help these people, as Canada helped our fathers and grandfathers." John nodded at the color party, who uncased and shook out the standards, parading them in front of the brigade before coming to a stop alongside John.

"Most of you have heard of these flags and some of you may have seen them, but now all of you will see them. The Red Ensign is the color of our country, the other the color of your forefathers, now changed to suit our new status as citizens of Canada. This is who we are. Our fathers and grandfathers earned the right to these ribbons in Afghanistan and Africa. You will earn them here in Syria."

As John paused for a moment to gather his thoughts, Lawrence looked at the two flags. The one on the right was a red field with a Union Jack in the top corner and the Canadian Coat of Arms in the bottom opposite. The other was blue, yellow and red horizontally stripped. In the center was a large maple leaf, to the left a German eagle, to the right a Russian bear and on the top a beaver. From the top of the staff hung two yellow streamers, battle honors from previous times. The color was old and patched, but still bright and full.

Performing the sign of the cross, John continued. "God grant us your protection for what we are about to receive. Help us achieve our goal with as little bloodshed for ourselves and our enemies as possible. And should you deem to take us, make us a place at Odin's side in Valhalla to serve you in the afterlife."

Each trooper made the sign of the cross in the old manner, kissing their fingers at the end.

Looking over at the Arabs, John saw them rising to their feet after the prayer. "Now you know it is not sporting to take the enemy so completely by surprise," he continued with a sly grin on his face. "A tribute to the King, I think."

Four thousand voices broke into "God Save The King" singing slow and harmoniously, not as the English sang, but more like the Russians. The anthem was finished with three rousing *hurrahs* and each trooper marched to their jumping-off positions. Armored car engines were fired up. John marched up the hill, stopping before the colors would be seen by the other side, and began to sing; the tune was quickly picked up by the brigade. It was a slow song in Russian, that low sorrowful sound that came from the heart and stirred the soul. It had a faint beat like a horse's galloping hoofs, and slowly the song sped up and increased in volume. Soon the very ground was vibrating as each trooper sang in perfect harmony that rousing Russian ballad, and as their leader slowly raised his hand, four thousand hands worked four thousand bullets into breeches and the gunners slammed home their munitions and drivers revved their engines nervously. Even the Arabs were struck by the sound as they mounted their horses, barely keeping the beasts under control, running in circles, waving their rifles over their heads and shouting their war cries.

Every eye was on the man at the head of the singing group: the song came faster and faster, then *stopped* – and the hand fell. With a mighty *hurrah*, the troopers were on their feet streaming over the hill, the ten field guns and twenty mortars spitting out their shells in unison as the first armored car went screaming over the hill, pennants now flying high. Artillery spotters and their radio men set up positions to direct fire and their leader stood calmly on the top of the hill under the flying flags, binoculars to his eyes, in full view of the enemy below. The Bears and Eagles had just joined the Great War.

It was over almost before it began. The first artillery shells had caught the Turks out in the open, trying to see where the singing was coming from. The next, now directed, took out most of their artillery and machine guns, and by the time the dismayed troops had been able to reach their trenches, the armored cars were spitting bullets out of the Lewis and Vickers guns mounted on them as fast as they could be fired. Cutting down men like a mower in wheat. Few if any return shots were fired and the sight of infantry approaching with fixed bayonets put paid to any heroics from the defenders. The few who tried to escape to the north were met by the ten armored cars in that direction and, after a few were killed, they surrendered. Not so lucky were the troops who tried to escape to the south: these were met by the Arabs, who were in no mood to accept surrender.

John motioned for Lawrence to join him as he mounted his truck, the two standards now affixed to the sides of the armored body. John instructed the driver to take his time and told the radio operator to tell the artillery to pack up and the transport trucks to form up and follow. Reaching the center of the enemy camp, the vehicle stopped and John dismounted, an under officer escorting a Turkish officer to him.

"But we were told the Russians had signed a treaty," the man said in Russian. "Why are you Cossacks attacking us?"

"That would be because we are not Russians," John replied in the same language.

"No," said another voice in a German uniform. "They are Canadians, and we are lucky to be alive."

"You are surrendering your position?" John asked.

"Yes, yes," replied the Turk. "Call off your Arabs; they are killing my men."

"Unfortunately, they are not my Arabs," John said. "Perhaps the major here can gain some control over them. Major," John continued in English to Lawrence. "If you would be so good as to take that armored vehicle there over to your allies and get them to stop killing those prisoners of theirs that would be appreciated."

As Lawrence left to try and gain control of the Arabs, John took a look at the German officer.

"Well, Colonel," he said in German. "It would appear that we caught you napping."

"You Canadians," the man said. "We can never figure you out. You don't follow the rules. I thought I had seen the last of you when they transferred me here."

"Well you are now a guest of the British army," John said. "If you will excuse me, I have matters to attend to. Call up HQ," he told his radio operator as the German moved out of earshot. "Tell them we have achieved our objective and are awaiting further instructions. I also want a butcher's bill as soon as possible. Oh, a bottle of vodka would be nice as well."

As his commanders came in to file their reports, he poured them each a glass of the fiery smooth beverage and they all stood around laughing in relief and talking loudly about how well their troopers had performed.

"Sir, our only casualties appear to be a flat tire and broken wheel," reported his radioman. This comment made the gathered officers laugh even more heartily, while their commander sat down on a chair and, taking his hat off, ran a shaking hand through his sweat-soaked hair.

"Thank God," he said quietly; his commanders saw his quiet mood and the joking stopped. The old sergeant major walked over and filled John's glass, patting him on the shoulder.

"Tell your troopers I am proud of them," he said, "and get them ready to move out. Once the enemy figures out they have lost this position, they will come back for it. I want to be gone before then."

The RSM sat down beside him after the officers had left, pouring himself a drink in the process.

"It was a good first blooding," the veteran said. "Better than we got in Afghanistan and way better than what you faced in Africa."

"We got lucky," John said. "It won't happen again."

"Probably not," the grizzled veteran agreed. "They did well though and now they know they can do it. Not one trooper faltered: they all crossed the line and did their duty. There were more than a few rounds shot our way, you know."

John nodded, as the radio operator handed him a message. "They want us to hit the enemy they are facing in the rear as soon as we can," he said after reading it. "Only to be expected I guess. Gather as many weapons from the enemy as you can find. Ruin those field guns and see how many maxims and ammunition for them we can salvage. Wreck the rest. Then get the troops mounted up. Tell Lawrence I want to see him and send for the enemy commanders."

"Gentlemen," John addressed the enemy commanders. "Sadly I have received orders to move on. I have neither the resources nor the time to care for prisoners. We will leave you one Maxim with five hundred rounds and one hundred rifles with one hundred rounds each to protect yourselves from the Arabs, but not enough to cause anyone any real problems. RSM, see to it if you please."

"Who is that man and who are you people?" the Turkish colonel asked, as John walked away.

"That is General Bekenbaum," answered the RSM. "We call ourselves the regiment. You will not find us on any orders of battle or depth charts. We were born to fight, trained to fight, love to fight. But we would rather not fight. Pray thanks to your God that you lived to say you fought us, and ask Him that you never face us again."

As the regiment mounted their trucks and drove away, the Turk turned to the German.

"They speak German, their leader has a German name, they fly a Cossack flag and sing in Russian," the Turk said. "Who are these people?"

"They come from a land wilder than the steppes of Russia," said the German. "His father is an English and a Russian earl. His mother a Russian baroness of Cossack blood. His grandfather was a famous German general and baron. They are Christian and Jew, Muslim and non believers. They take anyone who wants to be free and is willing to fight for it. They fight like demons and are generous to a fault. They call themselves Canadians and he is right. Pray in thanksgiving, and that you never meet them in the field of battle again."

John was standing in the open cab of his truck watching his well-trained troops operate as they had been trained. While the main group maintained a steady twenty miles an hour, four armored cars would rush ahead to a prominent point and spread out looking in all directions for enemies. They stayed in that position until the main group had passed them and then moved up to the front again. As the lead armored cars reached the watching group another four cars would break forward to start the sequence all over again. This way the main group was covered at all times without stopping, able therefore to cover much more ground.

John spotted four specks in the air and yelled back down into the body of the truck. "Four airplanes, eleven o'clock high: if they start to strafe us knock them out of the sky," he yelled. "Give me the battalion mike." He cleared his throat and spoke into the mike. "I know you can hear me on this net. If those RAF fools strafe my column I will blow their asses out of the sky, and if I miss some, I will finish them off when I get back to base."

Four cars per side pulled out and stopped, their Lewis guns trained on the now-diving airplanes. Lewis guns on all the vehicles also trained on the nearing airplanes and, as the first airplane opened fire, every Lewis and Vickers machine gun in the formation opened up on the airplanes, spraying hundreds of bullets per minute at the approaching menaces. The first one literally disintegrated, the one behind catching fire. The third and fourth broke off, with the last one trailing smoke and the third, its pilot slumped over.

An hour later, the point armored cars, while in the process of cresting the next hill, suddenly stopped and hurriedly backed down until they could not be seen from the other side. Five men from each car hurried out and spread themselves along the hilltop, lying prone, with weapons at the ready. John told the radioman to signal a halt, in column, to the rest of the brigade, and continued up the hill to reach the first car, the commander standing on the running board. No words were necessary, as small-arms fire and outgoing shelling could be heard – a lot of it. John jumped down from his car and crouching came up to the firing line his men had set up just below the crest of the hill.

The reverse slope of the hill had a gradual descent to the flood plain about one hundred feet below, and the view from the top was excellent. Less than five hundred yards away and to the left was a line of gun batteries, firing outbound as fast as they could. In front of that, a large mass of infantry was forming behind a system of only two trenches. The trenches were full of infantry, shoulder to shoulder, crouching down, heads beneath the trench lips. About one hundred yards in front of that trench, khaki uniforms could be seen, some lying prone and firing, others digging in like mad fiends and still others lying dead or wounded all around. Shells were bursting in and above the ground. Another formation was beginning its run and inbound shells from British guns were bursting around the trench system, occasionally making a direct hit.

A tap on John's shoulder broke his concentration and he looked left; the trooper next to him pointed further left and John could see an enemy observation point two hundred yards that way. The observers, to busy looking forward and directing fire out bound, to have observed them. Sliding back down below the crest of the hill, he made the spread out and dismount hand signal and the trucks pulled out of column, disgorging their troopers, who rapidly formed skirmish lines, set up mortars and field guns or began to set up a dressing station behind the guns.

John ran over to the first armored car and addressed the commander. "There is an enemy observation point two hundred yards to the left," he said. "I want you to take these four cars and knock it out. Once that is done, start directing fire on the field guns below. Go!"

The other commanders came rushing up, artillery spotters with their radiomen right behind them.

"I want suppression fire on the troops massing in the open, ASAP," he ordered the spotters, who sprinted up to the crest of the hill and began hammering out firing coordinates to the gun crews in the rear.

"Bears to form defensive fallback positions at the crest of the hill and another by the truck laager. All Lewis and Vickers guns to the top now; all Eagles, spread out along the top and wait for my signal to assault. Armored cars to assault all field guns they can see and support ground troops thereafter, they go now! Eagles will assault until the front trench line is clear," John ordered, and troopers sprinted to comply. Lewis guns erupted to the left, clearing the enemy observation point then firing down at the field guns, thirty armored cars in line abreast roared up and over the hill, stopping halfway down, Lewis and Vickers guns hammering away as mortar rounds started impacting on the massing soldiers in the open, followed by air bursts of shrapnel shells from the field guns opening up above enemy heads, flinging bodies everywhere.

"Sir," his radioman said. "I have informed the Brits that we are here and beginning an assault. They said they would stop theirs and wait until they hear from us."

"Wonder how long that will take to reach the troops on the ground," mused John aloud.

"It was their forward CP I contacted, sir," said the radioman. "I found their frequency and contacted them direct."

By now, John had gone back to the hill crest and could see that the khaki figures had indeed stopped their advance, while the ones in front were still laying down fire and digging like mad. Shortly after, the shells coming from the big guns to the rear stopped impacting the trench line and heads in the enemy trenches started to pop up, looking around.

"Two last rounds then stop; be ready for support," John told the artillery spotter, and, looking left and right to ensure the Eagles were ready, he raised his right arm. When the last of the second rounds were in the air he brought his hand sharply down and the Eagles poured over and down the hill with a mighty roar. The Bears opened up with every rifle into the disorganized formations below and the armored cars shifted fire into the packed men in front, clearing wide swaths in their lines as two and sometimes three men at a time were impacted by the .303 bullets smashing through tight packed bodies.

The infantry troopers opened fire from the hip as they advanced, felling still more, and the fire from the bears was deadly. Soon, enemy soldiers were turning to return fire, but it was too little too late, and masses began to move toward the safety of filled trenches, while EBB bayonets and bullets started their deadly work. The armored cars moved forward, turning sideways to the trenches to mow down the shoulder-to-shoulder Turks.

Even before the Turks began to throw down their weapons and go to their knees, empty arms raised high, John had sent the armored cars a message to stop firing, and officers were blowing their whistles, calling a halt to the slaughter. The regiment had not gotten away unscathed this time: khaki-clad bodies were lying amongst the Turks, and stretcher bearers already pelting downhill to attend to wounded. One armored car was smoking from a lucky grenade that had somehow gotten inside through a gun port and exploded.

Taking a deep breath and exhaling, John glanced up and saw that the sun was heading toward the western horizon, and the action, which had started just past noon and seemed to last but moments, had actually taken the better part of three hours. Hearing bagpipes in the distance, John looked ahead and saw all the British troops waving their rifles above their heads and cheering. The men in the armored cars not manning Lewis guns were standing on the roofs of the vehicles, bowing to the Brits and doing Cossack squats, legs flying and bouncing in celebration as the surrendering Turks were rounded up by watchful Eagles, rifles with reddened bayonets pointing at the prisoners.

"OK, boys." John spoke to the nearest of the Bears' officers. "Back to the trucks, have the casualty station moved down here and have the cooks start setting up – the troopers will be hungry. See about ammo and fuel states for everyone; we may have to bug out in a hurry."

As the officer hurried away to implement the orders, John's radioman came up.

"Colonel Makarov is deploying four cars to scout the rear and ten to set up observation posts along the hill," the man said. "He is also setting up firing lines to secure the hill in case of a counter attack."

John nodded that he had received the message and took the proffered water bottle from the RSM.

"Thought you had taken a hit at first," the RSM said, "but it was just your canteen."

That's when John noticed his left leg was wet, and pulling out his water bottle he saw it had received a through and through hit. "Holy shit. I didn't even notice they were shooting back."

"Well, if you must stand in full view of the enemy, John," said the old veteran, "do try and keep moving. At least make them work for it instead of giving them a stationary target."

Several of the troopers standing near them had overheard the conversation and saw John looking at the canteen, and were nudging those who hadn't seen it and talking into their ears.

"Well at least it will give the lads something to talk about," said John. "Look at the dumb brass hat, almost got himself killed he did."

His whiney voice, almost mimicking a five-year-old

whining to his mother, brought laughter to both men, and the troops only shook their heads.

"Look at the general," they said. "Almost got his leg shot off and he's laughing about it." Then they too started laughing and joking about the stupid things they had done, relieving the pent-up horror they had just witnessed and taken part in.

"They want to see you at the CP, General," said his over-worked radioman.

"Just as soon as I can find a way across the trench lines I will," John replied. "I would like the butcher's bill before I leave. RSM, see if you can round up some bridging material so we can get at least a truck over those trenches," he said, and the RSM hurried away, gathering troopers who looked like they weren't busy on the way.

Looking at his radio operator scribbling away copying messages and responding to them, John called over his aide.

"See if you can get two or three more radio operators to help poor Peter out there," he ordered. "Another lesson learned: this is to much for one man to handle."

Trucks began streaming over the hill; the first ones had the medical teams and even before their tents were up nurses and doctors were beginning the grisly task of saving wounded young men from both sides.

His aide handed him a message sheet; he was white as a ghost and trembling slightly.

A hundred and twenty dead, three hundred wounded, status of wounded unknown at this time. Five of the dead from one armored car, vehicle still operational. One armored car out of action due to engine failure, the report stated.

John closed his eyes and took a deep breath. More dead and wounded in this one action than in all the history of the regiment, he thought. One hundred and twenty mothers mourning lost sons. Looking about the field, he saw the Brits were taking control of the prisoners and made a snap decision.

"Sound the recall and fall in if you please," he yelled at his radio operator. "Break out the colors and have the troops form up facing the battlefield," he told his aide, then strode to ten yards from the top of the hill.

All the troopers except those engaged in helping the wounded double timed up the hill and formed up in their troops and squadrons. John kept his back to them while they got organized, looking at the battlefield, getting control of his emotions. The RSM came to his side, came to attention and saluted.

"Regiment is assembled, sir," he said quietly.

John took a deep breath, tugged down his jacket and squared away his battered Stetson before facing the RSM and returning his salute, then both men performed parade ground turns, simultaneously ending up facing the regiment.

"REGIMENT, ATTENTION," bellowed the RSM. "REGIMENT, SALUTE."

John waited a moment before he returned the salute, his right arm coming up to his forehead smartly. He held it for a second, then smartly pulled his hand down, placing it behind his back and shifting his feet to the at ease position, placing his left hand at the small of his back and grasping his right.

"REGIMENT, AT EASE," the RSM bellowed and the regiment shifted rifles and feet to the at ease position too, placing their left arms behind them, right arms holding grounded rifles at an angle to their bodies.

John turned his head from the left of the formation to the right and, as his eyes fell on the visible gaps in the Eagles formations, he visibly faltered, before moving on to the end of the formation. Returning his gaze to the center of the formation, he began to speak, moving his head to engage as many of the troopers' gazes as he could.

"Brothers and sisters, for the first time in sixteen years, the regiment has gone to battle. For the first time in its history it has engaged in not just one major battle, but two in one day. You have done well and you can take pride in joining and adding to your heritage. You are a credit to your ancestors and to your training."

He stopped then, looking at the pride in his troopers as they all stood tall, many with grins.

"You have faced death and embraced it. You have faced fear and overcome it. You have done your duty and have earned the right to wear that maple-leaf badge on your cap, the word *Canada* on your shoulder and the bears and eagles on your collars.

"Now I want you to look at the field before you. Take a good hard and long look." John paused then and saw the smiles start to leave. Raising his voice to almost a shout, he continued, pointing his right arm behind him. "That is what happens when you don't do your duty! That is what happens when you let your guard down! Not one job we do here is unimportant, no matter how dull or boring or seemingly pointless.

"Because they did not guard their rear, they died! Because they did not send out patrols, they died! Because they felt safe, they died! Because they were over confident, they died!"

He looked at the formations sternly, leaving his arm

pointing behind him for several seconds, letting it sink in. Bringing his arm back in, he removed his Stetson with his left hand and went down on one knee, making the sign of the cross with his right hand. Immediately the regiment en masse followed suit.

"Heavenly Father, I thank You for giving me the courage to lead these warriors. I thank You for choosing to guide them and protect them, in this their hour of need. We ask You to guide our healers to help the wounded and to help all the wounded endure and heal. We ask You to bring solace to the families of all the fallen." John finished with the sign of the cross and stayed, head bowed on one knee.

Just then the wind picked up and blew both flags out. John gazed at the blue yellow and red flag with the crest and read the motto underneath and for the first time felt the words. "*Determination Against All Odds*," he said. Then he stood and, putting his Stetson on his head, pointed at the flag and said it again louder. This time, some of the regiment repeated it. Then he raised his right arm above his head and clenched his fist punching the air and yelled it out. This time the whole regiment yelled it out and again he punched his arm in the air and they yelled it out again, then again and they screamed it out for the final time. John waited for a few seconds for them to settle down, then broke out in a grin.

"Enough of this shit," he yelled, "I'm thirsty, who's got the vodka?!"

A roar broke out as the RSM handed John a flask and the regiment broke formation, friends hugging each other and patting backs.

The RSM turned John around to face the battlefield, where upturned faces were watching them. He nodded at the RSM and grabbed the national colors, while the RSM grabbed the regimental ones, and both men began to swirl them about themselves. A mighty roar erupted from the khaki uniforms below, rifles and fists punching the air, and soon Australian and New Zealand ensigns were waving and finally a full Union Jack.

Jamming the standards back in the ground the two men left them in care of the grinning color guard and headed for the truck chosen as John's transport.

"Those poor bastards needed that," said the RSM, nodding at the Commonwealth troops, still cheering.

"There hasn't been much to cheer about for the last three years," John said. "This was their victory as much as ours."

Then he saw a group of officers standing to one side, under armed guard, but still armed. Switching directions, John marched over to them; noticing one was a lieutenant general in the Imperial German Army, he stopped two paces in front of him, came to attention and saluted.

"Sir, Brigadier General Bekenbaum of the Canadian Army at your service, sir!" John barked out in High German.

The surprised German officer came to attention and returned the two Canadians' salute.

"Lieutenant General von Bekenbaum of the Imperial German Army," the German said in British-accented English. "It would have been nice to meet a relative under better circumstances."

"Life does that sometimes," John replied.

Saluting, a Turkish officer addressed John. "General El Mati at your service, General," he said as John returned his salute. Waving his hand, he took his regimental standard and handed it to John, who accepted it and handed it to the RSM.

"I surrender my soldiers to your care, sir," the Turk said.

"And I mine," said the German, waving his standard bearer over to give the RSM it as well.

"Your people fought well and bravely," said John.

"If we had known you sneaky Canadians were in the area, it might have been different," said the German.

Spotting some high-ranking British officers heading

their way, John decided to cut the conversation off. "Perhaps, then again, perhaps not," he replied with a grin. After a final salute, he and the RSM went to his truck, tossed the captured colors to the men in the rear and jumped in. John motioned the driver to take off before he had to talk to the British officers.

Chapter Two

Planks had been placed across the two trenches and they negotiated them safely; it was more difficult negotiating around the shell holes in front of the trenches, but eventually they made their way to the rear of the British lines and were directed to the command post.

Walking into the large tent, accompanied by his aide though, the Brits did not allow non-coms into staff meetings, John walked in on the end of a heated debate.

"I told you, Allenby, I told you these tactics would work. We should have been using them long ago," said an earnest brigadier general to the overall commander.

"Yes I suppose I have been shown," replied Allenby. "The results were definitely impressive. All right, draft a plan and I will have a look at it. You can't have the EBB, though: home office has other plans for them."

Dismissing the brigadier, Allenby spotted John and waved him over. "Speak of the devil," he said. "Very impressive, Bekenbaum. We could have used your regiment in France and Gallipoli."

"We may have been effective at the outbreak of war in Europe," replied John. "Not now and definitely not at

Gallipoli. Our tactics are more suited to this type of terrain and to a war of movement. We would not be very effective in static warfare, not unless some kind of breakout could occur first."

"Well, we are going to give it a go nevertheless," Allenby replied, nodding to the back of the departing brigadier. "He seems to think he will beat the Turks single-handed."

"What does he have for equipment?" John asked.

"Forty Rolls Royce armored cars and one hundred trucks," answered Allenby. "He will be backed up by two battalions of lancers and two of infantry."

"Sir, we are completely motorized," said John. "Not to criticize, but the type of tactics we rely on, speed is of the essence. Being held up by infantry and cavalry will be a handicap. Not to say you won't be effective, just not as effective."

"Why do you say that?" the commander asked.

"We have been developing these tactics for over ten years now and today I realized we have to modify still more," answered John. "Our tactics are based on the tactics our people have been using successfully for centuries, adapting them to motorized transport instead of horses."

At that point, two officers dressed in British uniform

and wearing turbans came into the room and saluted.

"Ah, right on time, gentlemen," said Allenby. "I am just about to give the general his new orders. Bekenbaum, the Home Office, in recognition of your regiment's unique abilities and past experience, is ordering you to Afghanistan. These gentlemen are from the region bordering it and will be accompanying you. They are well-trained lancers. The route you will be traveling is behind the lines and we need you to do as much disruption as possible along the way. The Russians are expected to sign a peace treaty with the Germans any day now and we must convince the Turks that we can hit them anywhere we wish at any time. They are wavering, Bekenbaum: a few more disasters and they will be out of it."

"Lancers, sir?" John said.

"You think we are not good enough for you?" said the Indian major indignantly.

"I assure you, Bekenbaum," Allenby said. "These are first-rate troops. They have proven themselves many times in this campaign."

"I am sure, sir," John said. "One question for the major then?"

Allenby gestured to continue.

"I plan on covering one hundred miles per day at a

minimum," John said, looking directly at the major. "After the second day, when all your horses are dead, you will be useless to me and I will not be stopping for you. What then, major?"

The two Indian officers looked at each other.

"One hundred miles a day?" the major asked. "Impossible."

"My father averaged thirty miles a day for over a month getting to and from Afghanistan," said John. "With his support wagons. They said that was impossible too. Gentlemen, we traveled fifty miles two days ago. Today we fought two engagements and moved thirty miles between engagements and the day is not over yet. If we had to, we could do it again tomorrow. You think about that. General, I must see to my men," he said to Allenby. "Please have whatever maps you have of the area sent to me. I will be sending you a list of supplies we will need. If you come up with a way for the lancers to come with us, they know where they can find us."

Saluting Allenby, John left the tent. "Bloody Brits," he said, jumping into the truck. He waved the driver to take them back to their camp and was already thinking on other things before they had left the command post area.

His command tent and command support tents were

assembled and waiting by the time he arrived. Climbing out of the truck he went to the radio tent and addressed the officer in charge.

"Assemble the big rig," he ordered. "I want to contact home base as soon as we can."

"We'll try, sir," the captain said.

John nodded and headed for his own tent. The lieutenant acting as his aide handed him what turned out to be the casualty list. The dead had risen to one hundred twenty-five, as five men had died from their wounds. Fifty of the wounded would have to be sent home because of missing limbs or worse; the others would have to stay behind and might as well be sent home as well. By the time they recovered, the regiment would be out of reach.

John looked at the names on the lists. He had grown up with some, knew the elder brothers or sisters of the rest. The whole regiment did. As he was thinking of the heartbreak the news would bring back home, he laid his head back on the edge of the chair he was sitting on and in seconds was fast asleep.

"Sir, general sir," a voice said, an arm shaking his shoulder. "They have made contact home, sir," the lieutenant said once he was sure John was awake.

John stood hurriedly, making sure he had the casualty

list, he jammed his battered Stetson on his head and rushed to the radio tent. Motioning the radio operator away, he took up the man's earphones and placed them on his head. Placing the casualty list in front of him, he took up the Morse key and began transmitting in their private cypher.

"*Eagle base, eagle base, this is beaver one, over.*"

"*Beaver one, eagle base, two by four, over.*"

"*Eagle base, beaver one, three by five, long trans, over.*"

"*Beaver one eagle base ak long trans when ready, over.*"

"*Eagle base, beaver one, this day regiment partakes first engagement at these coordinates begins at six am local regiment destroys eight heavy guns destroys or captures ten maxim guns inflicts heavy enemy casualties captures then releases eight k plus prisoners no friendly casualties regiment then travels thirty miles to engage in second action at these coordinates en route regiment is attacked by four friendly aircraft regiment destroys two and heavily damages another two no regiment casualties at noon local regiment begins second engagement regiment destroys or captures ten batteries heavy guns and unknown maxim guns regiment inflicts heavy casualties on enemy positions combined Turk and Kraut forces surrender four pm local at this time unknown number of enemy casualties or prisoners but extensive Gen von Bekenbaum one of the prisoners wait one. ... Eagle base, beaver one, ready to transmit further traffic, over."*

"Beaver one, eagle base ak further traffic, over."

"Eagle base, beaver one, EBB casualties as follows five officers one hundred twenty other ranks confirmed KIA twenty officers two hundred other ranks confirmed WIA how read will confirm names, over."

"Beaver one, eagle base, three by four steady, ak further traffic, over."

"Eagle one, beaver one, casualties as follows."

John then transmitted all the names. The radio tent was quiet except for the humming of the machines and the noise of the generators powering the equipment. Each of the radio operators had been following the transmission and listening to the names, and it began to sink in – the losses they had sustained.

"Beaver one, eagle one ak receipt casualties, Bald Eagle sends his prayers and well done, over."

"Eagle base, beaver one, God bless the King, God bless Canada, and God bless the regiment, beaver one out."

"Beaver one, eagle base Bald Eagle repeats beaver one again well done and God bless, eagle base out."

"Let the troops know the commander said well done boys," John said. "Break this down; I'm off for bed."

On the other side of the world it was morning.

Andreas looked at the names on the list and sighed. Always the brightest and the best, he thought.

"I'll take this copy with me," he told the radio operator. "Have the names printed out properly. I want to contact the families myself. Under no circumstances is anyone to divulge this information until all the families have been contacted, is that clear?"

Back at the house, Andreas passed the long message to Johannes, who then as he finished reading each page, passed it on to Elizabeth.

"I'll get the unit commanders to let the families know and have them brought in," said Johannes.

"My God, they drove thirty miles and two engagements in one day," said Andreas. "It sounds like they destroyed at least two divisions and with only four hundred of our own out of action."

John, the task done, put down the headphones, thanked the operators and walked out of the tent into the clear moonlit night, putting both hands in the crook of his back and arching it as far as he could while twisting his head left and right. The camp was strangely quiet: troopers huddled with their messmates, only occasional laughter coming here and there. He pulled one of his limited cigars out of his jacket breast pocket as he walked, vainly searching for a match, when beside him a flare from a match appeared and was put to the end of the cigar. As soon as it was burning the match was blown out.

"No, sense giving a sniper a chance," said the RSM. "The troops did well today."

"We got lucky," John said.

"A little luck is always welcome," the RSM said. "Better training, better weapons and better tactics, more like. It was the same in Afghanistan. They used methods that worked in the last war and we used new methods. The result was the same."

"You were in Afghanistan?" asked John.

"Raw recruit, turned eighteen about a week before the fight," said the RSM slowly, as his mind went back to that day.

"We stood there in two lines of five hundred, dressed in red uniforms to make us look like the Brits. They came at us at a full gallop. my God the earth was trembling from the hoofbeats. My knees started to shake, and, as the order came to present, my rifle was bouncing all over the place. Your father rode his horse down the line calm as you please, making a joke about leaving some for the Afghanis to kill, to be neighborly, then he rode to the back of the line and, just like you did now, lit a cigar. The enemy was coming hard, bunching up; they knew some of them would die, but that we would only get two shots off before they had us. They started to sing, sensing victory, but at three hundred yards your father yelled out fire and the front rank let loose until they were empty, then we in the rear rank fired while they reloaded. On they still came, jumping the mounds of dead and dying. Then the Bears opened up on both flanks. I reloaded three times and was down to my last two rounds when they broke. That's how close it came, John: we all knew we were dead – then they broke. God, I was scared shitless.

"Your father killed the two who broke through our lines. Before that he was calmly riding up and down giving encouragement. That more than anything kept me going. He felt we would do it and wasn't worried, so I kept going."

Both men stood smoking in quiet for a while.

"Just like you today, John," the RSM went on. "Both times you stood, watching and calmly giving directions, in full view, mindless of the bullets flying around you. The troops saw and it calmed them down. If you could be calm, so could they. Just like your father with me."

"I grew up hearing the inner circle talking of that fight," John said. "Like you and all of them, including my father, I was just as scared shitless as you and your troopers were."

"Any person that faces what we do and says he isn't scared is lying or a psychopath," said the RSM.

Agreeing, John took another pull on the cigar and reminded the RSM that they would have to replace the Eagles lost that day.

"Selection process will be in four days," said the RSM.

"Thank you. Give the grenaded car to the crew that blew their engine," John said. "Cleaning up the mess and seeing the damage dents on the inside might remind them what will happen if they do it again."

"What's all this about some Indian lancers joining us?" the RSM asked.

"Not going to happen unless they can find some transport," John said. "Then they have to pass selection, just like everybody else."

"Burial detail is briefed on what you want," said the RSM. "They have gathered enough materials to do the job."

"Good. I don't want anybody digging up our dead," John said. "Enough for one day. Get some sleep: I need you in the morning and I have had enough for one day myself."

We all need you, young Bekenbaum, thought the RSM as he watched John enter his tent and the light go out. You're the only thing that is likely to get us through all this. Then he, like his commander, hit his cot and was asleep as soon as he closed his eyes.

It was almost noon when John's aide woke him.

"General, lunch is ready," he said. "You have a thirteen hundred meeting."

John grunted and rolled out of the cot, blinking at the bright daylight and feeling the heat of the tent. His batman and aide had laid out a clean uniform for him and the batman was waiting with razor in hand. John stripped off the old sweat-soaked uniform and donned the fresh undergarments and fatigue pants, then sat and allowed the batman to shave his two-day growth of beard. After that was done, the batman helped him with his high-top laced boots while John donned the shirt and did the buttons. Sticking his uniform brimmed cap under his arm, John walked out of the tent and to the table set up under the tent fly in front. Accepting a cup of coffee and cigarette, he sat down, took a sip and lit up. He began reading the pile of reports laid out in front of his chair.

The table had been set for four, but for the moment John was alone, reading and signing off on ammunition expenditures and resupply requirements, fuel purchase and resupply, as well as rations and medical supplies. He had just completed the last task when Colonel Makarov approached with the two commanding officers of the prisoners. John stood up and the men exchanged salutes, then John motioned his three guests to sit and the lunch dishes were served. As they ate and exchanged pleasantries, a British colonel and major came storming up to the table.

"What do you bloody Canadians think you're about?" demanded the colonel without preamble. "Who gave you permission to take captured Maxims and ammunition and powder charges?"

John slammed his hand on the table and rose from his chair so fast he knocked it over; he caught himself reaching for his Colt's handle, then remembered it was still inside the tent. The gesture was not lost on the British major, who had been standing at attention, saluting the whole time.

"Colonel, the articles of war state that disrespect to a superior officer in the field is punishable by court martial," John said, his voice barely audible.

The colonel now realized what he had done and came

to attention, saluting. "My apologies, General."

John stared at the man for a full minute, making him hold the salute all the while, before finally returning it.

"At ease," John ordered. "My apologies for my behavior, Major, I am afraid I let my emotions get a hold of me for a moment and you received the brunt of it through no fault of your own. Now, Colonel, I captured those weapons, not you. Be thankful I have no use for the heavy guns I left, or you wouldn't have those either. I am also taking all the petrol the enemy has and if that does not sit well with you, I suggest you take it up with General Allenby. You are dismissed, Colonel. Major, a word, if you please?"

John waited until the sulking colonel was stalking away, out of earshot.

"Major, would you do me a favor by taking these reports to your commander?" John asked, handing the man the large pile of reports he had earlier dealt with. "The general is waiting for them and it will save me sending one of my officers down there. We are all a little busy right now."

"My pleasure, sir," said the Major, accepting the bundle of papers.

"Your name please, Major?" asked John.

"Major Alex Hood, Coldstream Guards, on loan to the General sir," the major replied.

"Very well, Major Hood," said John, saluting sloppily, dismissing the man. "Please enjoy the remainder of this wonderful day."

"Thank you, sir," said the major, returning the salute and marching away toward the main British camp.

"The British are ever so arrogant," von Bekenbaum said in German, while the Turk nodded in agreement.

"Almost as arrogant as you Germans," said John.

The Turk snorted the coffee he had just sipped through his nose at that comment, while John and Edward sat straight faced, watching the German smolder. "Me, I'm just a poor farmer, an amateur soldier – what do I know of all these things?"

"Armature?" asked the Turk. "What do you mean?"

"Not armature, *amateur*. You know, not professional. Why, didn't you know?" asked Edward, going along with John. "We are only a militia regiment, not a full time army unit at all."

"That is nonsense and you know it," said the German. "You are organized just like we are, you train just like we do. Why is it that you fight for these British and not for your fatherland? It is not right."

"I do not engage in politics," said John. "My country, like yours did you, asked me to serve, and it is my duty to do so, like you."

"Yes," agreed the Turk. "I have never met a British before this. We were to fight the Russians and to quell a rebellion out here. I thought your regiment was Russian – we hear you singing Russian songs at night."

"Most of us come from banished Germans who settled in a part of Russia controlled by the Don Cossacks," said Edward. "Some of us are Russian, some are English, some are Poles, some are Americans, some are even oriental. We call ourselves Canadians: most of us were born there, educated there and speak English first."

"But you owe allegiance to the Fatherland," said the German.

"Before you make me and yourself angry, cousin," said John quietly. "You should remember the facts not the propaganda you have been fed. We are Canadians; we owe allegiance to King George and the people of Canada. Amongst ourselves we may talk the old languages and follow the old traditions, but we are Canadians, and it would suit your people well to remember that.

"Now to the business at hand. We will be conducting a memorial service for all the fallen this evening. As the victor on the field, I am inviting you to participate. My whole regiment will be attending; whether you join us and in what numbers is up to you. Secondly, right now you are my prisoners and I am responsible for you. That will be changing soon, as the regiment will be sent on a new task and I will have to hand you over to the British.

"As a result, I will be releasing two field grade officers from each of your units. Firstly, to report to your governments the status of your capture. Secondly, to let your people know this. The regiment will be commencing operations in this theater. As yet I do not know where or for how long.

"Cousin," said John. "Please convey my respect to your parents and know this. None of this is personal. I would rather not be fighting my relatives. Unfortunately both our governments have made avoiding that impossible."

"If you say so," his cousin said, standing. "Now with your permission I will take my leave."

The RSM approached as the two officers were leaving under escort of a captain.

"Not very friendly, our cousin," the RSM, a Bekenbaum on his mother's side, said.

"Things have changed and not for the better in the fatherland," John said. "Are the arrangements made?"

"Yes, sir," the RSM said. "The Commonwealth units have been informed and your vehicles will be set up and ready when you need them. Was that wise, telling them our plans?"

"Our job as light cavalry is first to do reconnaissance and intelligence for the army," John said. "Secondly we are to disrupt supply routes and create havoc in the enemy rear. Yes I want them to know and after we hit them a few times, they will expend a lot of manpower trying to find and stop us. Clear?"

"Clear as mud, sir," the RSM said.

"Very well, thank you, RSM; carry on," John ordered, then scribbled a quick note to Allenby. "I think that having Major Hood join us as liaison officer would be a good thing; do you agree?" John said, handing the message to Edward.

"I will pass on the request, John," said Colonel Makarov, and once again John was left alone with his thoughts.

Chapter Three

"It's time, General," his batman announced, sticking his head past the tent flap.

"Right then," said John, "let's get on with it."

His batman, dressed in his formal blue uniform, entered the tent and waited for John to finish buttoning his dress uniform jacket and put his hands to the side to allow the aide to wrap the sword belt about his waist. It was not a British model cavalry or infantry officer's sword, but a traditional Cossack common trooper's sword. Instead of his normal shoulder holster, his Colt automatic pistol was now housed in a burnished leather holster on his right hip. Breaking with regimental tradition, John placed his highly burnished general officer's cap squarely on his head, the brim low over his eyes. The only decoration he was wearing was an Eagle on one collar and Beaver on the other. The maple leaf in the middle of his cap and text on his right shoulder proclaimed him a Canadian. The highly polished brass of the badging contrasted smartly with the dark-blue dress uniform.

"TENHUT!" bellowed the RSM as John exited the tent: the regiment had formed ranks, all in dress uniform and all without orders, in front of his quarters.

Returning the salute, John, flanked by the RSM on one side and Colonel Makarov on the other, marched to the right of the column. The regiment was given the command to turn left in columns of four, and, at the head of his troops and in front of the color party, John marched to where the battlefield cemetery was located. Breaking off from the regiment as he came abreast of his command truck, John waited until the troops had been ordered to halt and the colors had been affixed to either side of the vehicle, and the Union Jack placed on the middle of the roof. He then deftly climbed to stand behind the microphone waiting in the center of the roof in front of the Union Jack, overlooking the formations of troops ranged in front of him.

Before him in their regiments and battalions were ranged the Commonwealth troops, their national and battalion colors in front. To one side were the defeated Axis troops, while on the other was the only color of the formation, the regiment in their dress dark-blue uniforms, brass and fixed bayonets shining in the setting sun.

Among his troops, in a separate line in front, were his wounded, some on stretchers, all dressed in at least dress uniform jacket. The sight of these warriors come to honor their comrades put a lump in John's throat and, not for the last time that day, he had to swallow hard to stop from breaking down.

In front of his troops were two pits, ten feet deep, six feet wide, and one hundred and fifty feet long. At the bottom of each pit was stacked four feet of wood soaked in kerosene. As soon as the regiment was settled at ease, the grumbled mutter of engines was heard: twenty-five trucks escorted by unarmed men on each side slowly entered the field, coming to a stop in front of the pits. The regiment was called to attention as one hundred and twenty-five blanket-shrouded bodies were lovingly removed from the trucks and gently lowered by rope to lie shoulder to shoulder in the pits. The pallbearers then joined their troops and the regiment was put at ease, all eyes on John.

"Brothers and sisters in arms," he began, thankful the PA system worked as planned without any feedback.

"We are gathered here to honor our brave comrades. Comrades who shared our trials and tribulations, our joys and our sorrows. Comrades who gave their lives serving their country's call to arms, who stood shoulder to shoulder with us. Comrades who had wives and sweethearts, mothers and fathers, brothers and sisters and children who loved them and will miss them. This sentiment transcends country or nationality: under the eyes of God, we are all his children. God sees no difference in country or religion. God welcomes us all as his children and judges on not what our countries or religions do, but on what we do in our lives. Rejoice that, unlike those of us left to mourn, our comrades are with God, no longer subject to the whims of man and nature. I ask all here now to look into their hearts and remember your lost comrades and all they meant to you."

The silence was complete: not a bird could be heard and the wind stopped.

After a full minute, John motioned to his bugler. At first he was the only one sounding the Last Post, but soon he was joined by all the Commonwealth buglers. When the haunting lament was finished, the last note echoing off the hill, the bagpipes from the Highland regiments began their soulful sounds, and every ten seconds a gun fired its salute. John nodded at the RSM and dismounted the truck; grabbing two unlit torches, he and the RSM marched to the pits and the regiment came to attention.

"Brothers and sisters," John said, now in Russian. "I promise each and every one of you that as I cannot take you home alive, I will ensure that no one will desecrate your graves. Our comrades lying here will live on forever in our minds and in our hearts. Their names will be listed in the Regiment History, for all to see, for all time."

He nodded again to the RSM, who, lighting a match,

lit both of the torches.

"In the ancient traditions, I now commend the earthly remains of our fallen comrades to the stars."

John then began to sing, slow and low, the Don Cossack song as he approached the pits, the song quickly picked up by the rest of the regiment. He solemnly threw the torches one in each pit and strode back to join his regiment and called them to attention, saluting. The flames engulfed the bodies in the pits with a roar as the last of the twenty-one-gun salute was fired and the bagpipes held their last long note.

Unlike most of the times they sang this song, this time the regiment kept to the slow tempo, their massed chorus reflecting the sorrow they all felt. Once, twice they sang that sorrowful refrain as the flames began to rise high and the smoke from the bodies drifted skyward. Then the song began a third time, this time rising in volume and tempo, until it was as fast as a horse at a gallop and soon dancers could no longer hold themselves back and began the steps Cossacks were famous for, dancing in celebration of their fallen comrades' lives. The ridged lines broke down to form a circle of healing around the pits, rifles slung on backs as singers and dancers clapped their hands, keeping up with the wild beat, and as the troopers lost themselves in their dance and song. John quietly left the field, unnoticed but for the RSM, who shadowed him into the now moonlit night.

John had a few minutes of peace in the dark on the side of the hill they had made their assault from, away from the sounds and the light of the main camp. He was puffing on a cigar, lying on his back on the ground, head resting on hands behind it, when soft footfalls and one hand on his shoulder and another placing a flask in front of his face announced the arrival of visitors.

The flask held scotch and the three visitors, all generals, a Scot, an Australian and a New Zealander, sat with him on the hill. The four men sat in silence for a while, reflecting in their moment of peace, for once not troubled by decisions to be made, or orders to be given.

"Bloody hell," exclaimed the Scot, lowering the now empty flask. "You bloody colonials have drunk all the scotch."

"Typical Scot," said the Australian. "Doesn't bring any booze then bitches because we ran out."

"You could have stayed back with the Brits, you know," said the New Zealander. "They have lots of booze."

"Mebbe they do," said the Scot. "Bloody bastards charge you for it too. They're all too stuck-up for my liking anyway."

John held up a half-gallon jug he had by his side, and four tin cups.

"I was expecting company," he said, pouring the cups full. "Just not of such outstanding high and mighty quality."

"Ach," said the Scot, "always the high and god-almighty Can-eye-dians. To good for the likes of us, eh?"

"Speak for yourself, Scottie" said the Australian.

"All you bloody colonials stick together," retorted the Scot, taking a long draft from the cup and breaking out in a lung-searing cough. "That is good hooch," he said, shaking his head and grimacing.

"Stays down better after the first one," John said. "Mud in your eye." He raised his cup to his companions then shot the draught back in one go.

The rest of the group followed suit, and while they were recovering, John refilled the cups.

'Where did you lay ahold of this stuff?" asked the New Zealander.

"I believe this batch came from my mother's potato patch," answered John. "I'm not planning on asking where the next batch comes from."

"Potato patch?" asked the Scot. "Make sense, man."

"This wonder brew is called vodka and this particular batch was made from good old Canadian potatoes. When in the field, the boys always find something to make it with. I don't ask and they don't tell."

They all fell silent again.

"That was a good thing you did tonight," said the New Zealander. "This war will be over soon and it was right what you said: enemies will have to learn to live together again after all this."

"As far as the Turks go," said the Australian, "I can see it. Did you see how badly they are treated? Why, they are half starved."

"Och aye," the Scot agreed, "the Huns treat them worse than the Brits treat the Indians and that is bad enough."

"Speaking of the Huns," said the Australian. "You are showing an amazing amount of restraint, John. I must say I am impressed."

"Why, I meant what I said," John replied. "They are men called to duty just like us."

"Really? Even after they deliberately sent bombers to bomb one of your hospitals?" the Australian asked.

"What are you taking about?" asked John.

"You didn't know?" the New Zealander asked, and the three men looked at one another, shocked, before he continued. "You people do wonders at your field hospitals and the Huns are bloody scared of your troops. So they sent a bombing raid and bombed your hospital. Burned it down, killed a few of the wounded and some nurses. First we thought, well maybe it was a mistake or something. Then the Brits found out during interrogation of a shot-down pilot that it was a deliberately planned raid."

"Oh shit, when did that happen?" said John.

"Couple of weeks ago," said the Australian. "Nobody said anything? We thought you all knew."

"My aunt commands that hospital and my sister is a nurse there." John stood up in a rush. "Keep the bottle, I have to go."

"Get home base now!" John ordered as he burst into the radio tent, startling the men.

He paced the floor while the operators changed frequencies and started to try and get home base.

Finally they did and the radio operator took off his earphones handing them to John, who shook his head. He was too upset to handle the radio.

"I want the casualty report for the hospital in France," he said.

He deciphered the call to wait, listening to the tones of the loud speaker.

After ten minutes of waiting he asked if they still had

the station and received another wait reply.

Another ten minutes went by before the tones began.

"*Beaver base, eagle base. Eagle two send following. Colonel Bekenbaum, Major Bekenbaum wounded not critical. Captain Bekenbaum KIA. Over.*"

John took the key. "*Thank you, Mother, will tell regiment. God bless out.*"

"Please tell Colonel Makarov to ask General von Bekenbaum that I would like the pleasure of his company for lunch tomorrow," he asked the radio officer, and made his way out of the tent clutching the message form, passing by the three other generals, not seeing they were there.

"He took that rather hard," said the Scot quietly.

"Yes sir," said the young lieutenant in charge of the radios that night. "His aunt and cousin were wounded in that hospital and his sister killed."

John was awake before dawn the next morning. It was qualification day. Bears were competing for the open Eagle positions and anticipation was rampant in the camp. He was just finishing his coffee when he heard strange motors coming into camp and looked out to see a large number of battered British trucks, jammed with Indian soldiers and preceded by four Bentley armored cars that had seen better days. The procession came to a stop, and soldiers piled out of the vehicles and formed up into two groups. One group had Lee–Enfields grounded beside them, the other fifty had no weapons.

John rose and greeted the Indian colonel.

"I am glad you chose to join us, Colonel," John said.

"Thank you, General," the Colonel replied.

"You can explain the extra fifty men?" John asked.

"Yes sir, they are our support troops, sir."

"Ah, I see. Well you have read the rest of our requirements then?" John asked. "They apply to your support troops as well, of course."

"Support troops?" said the colonel. "That is unheard of."

"We are behind enemy lines and a long way from help. We have no noncombatants in the regiment, Colonel. Your people don't meet minimum standards, they don't come. That includes you and your officers. Now, your horses: are they trained for fire arms as well as the lance?"

"Sir, of course sir: they are the best mounts in this army, sir," the colonel replied proudly.

"I would ask you if I could borrow fifty of them for a short time, Colonel," John said.

"Certainly sir; tack as well?"

"That won't be necessary, just halters and shanks," replied John. "If one of your officers would escort a few of my men to retrieve them? RSM, front and center." He turned to the man and continued. "Delegate a few men to bring fifty horses here for the trials if you please? Also have some mechanics go over those trucks, will you?"

"A little show then?" said the RSM, and hurried off to carry out the orders.

"Stand your men down, Colonel," said John. "It will take a while to set up my test."

Then, calling over Colonel Makarov, John outlined what he wanted. Soon the thunder of hoofs announced the arrival of the horses and they were herded into a hastily set-up rope corral; willing hands grabbed halters and snapped on halter shanks, holding the animals steady.

The targets for this special test were set up halfway up the hill they had assaulted down and crowds of off-duty spectators eager for something new started to line the plain below the hill.

"Candidates front and center," the RSM yelled out at John's nod.

Five hundred men and women lined up at attention and John moved forward to address them.

"Candidates," he said. "I want fifty volunteers to

compete with the old rules. Those who pass will not have to compete using the new qualifications. Those who do not shall still be able to try the new qualifications. Decide among yourselves. You have ten minutes."

As he knew it would, it only took two minutes for them to decide. The Bears knew who among them were the best at the skills required. The fifty volunteers sprinted off to their tents and returned, buckling on swords as they ran, rifles bouncing on their backs.

"Keep your eyes on the blond, Colonel," John told the Indian colonel. "She's here as a nurse, but she's always been interested in combat. Her mother, two aunts and grandmother are very good at this test and she just barely missed the cutoff for combat in our trials before we left."

The blond in question had removed her campaign hat and was quickly, with practiced ease, braiding her long hair in a single braid that she tucked under her rifle at her back. That done, she put the Stetson back on, low, just above her eyebrows, and pulled the chin strap tight against her chin.

At a signal from the RSM, the horses were brought forward and a truck pulled out in a cloud of dust and drove a mile away, where troopers piled out and stuck fifty lances point first into the ground. Once that was done the RSM gave the order to mount and the fifty volunteers jumped onto the horses' bare backs and lined up.

The RSM pulled out his Colt and, looking at the line, fired a shot into the air – and the fifty were off in a cloud of dust and a thunder of hoofs.

As the others took off at a gallop, the blond held her mount back to a canter, so that by the time she reached the lances, the weaker horses were already tiring and she was the first one to reach the targets, her lance squarely hitting the first. Pulling the rifle from her back, she fired three rounds into the first one-hundred-yard target and ran past the twenty-five-yard targets, replacing the rifle back on her back, then turning the horse around, drew her pistol and rapid-fired the automatic into the twenty-five-yard targets. Letting her pistol dangle from her neck strap, she pulled out her sword and neatly decapitated a dummy head.

As expected, the rest of the volunteers completed the task within the allotted time, though the rest of them opted to dismount at the rifle and pistol targets to make sure of their shots.

The Indian colonel was yelling something in his own language, as were his troopers and most of the onlookers below.

"By Jove!" he said to John. "And bareback! If I had not seen it, I would not have believed it. She hit that target at a full run and *bareback*. Unbelievable!"

"Not so unbelievable," the blond, a major, said. "Grandfather did it twice as fast and John here did it faster still: he shot the pistol targets lying on the side of the horse, firing under its neck."

John just shrugged his shoulders, hugged his cousin and kissed her on both cheeks. He took his eagle off his collar and pinned it on hers.

"Now, Colonel, you and your people know what you're competing with," he said. "If you want your support troops to come along, you better hope they can pass the minimums. Now if you will excuse me, the major and I have something to discuss."

John drew his cousin aside, dreading what he was about to tell her – she was beaming and basking in the congratulations she was receiving. When he had her sit down, a look of concern crossed her, as she saw he had become serious and stayed standing, his arms and legs at the at ease position.

"Major Bekenbaum," John began solemnly. "It is my sad duty to inform you that Colonel and Major Bekenbaum were wounded in action in France and that Captain Bekenbaum was killed in that same action."

"Are you joking, John?" she asked. "They are serving

way behind the lines in a hospital. Mother and Susan? Katia was *killed?*"

"Not a joke, Chris," said John. "The Germans bombed the hospital. The report I received last night said Willy and Susan's wounds are not critical. That's all I know. It happened two weeks ago and I only just found out about it."

"Sir," said Colonel Makarov. "General von Bekenbaum, sir."

"Have a seat, General," John said. "You two stay, this is family business," he told the two Canadian officers. "General, two of your cousins have been wounded and one killed, all of them nurses, in a bombing raid on our hospital in France," John said.

Von Bekenbaum shrugged his shoulders. "It's war, things happen," he said.

John felt Christine stiffen beside him, and put a hand on her arm. "Bombing a clearly marked hospital full of wounded?" he asked. "You condone that behavior. That is against the Geneva Convention."

"You Canadians, always harping on the Geneva Convention," the German said. "The whole object of warfare is to defeat or cause the enemy to quit. Don't you understand that? How naive."

"I see," said John. "Well, General, thank you for your insight into how far the Germans have sunk in their desperation over failing to conquer the world. You have badly misjudged us once again, cousin. That act will only make us more determined to get this war over with, and I can assure you, sir, if you thought us hard to deal with before, the gloves are coming off now. I will be handing control of your troops to the British this afternoon. Good afternoon, General."

As the German was escorted away, a confused-looking British major and corporal descended from a Ford truck, their duffle bags tossed onto the ground behind them.

"So good of you to join us, Major," said John. "Colonel, the major and his batman will be assigned to one of the cars of my protection detail. Please see to that and issue them weapons and have them taken to the practice field for some instruction."

Turning to Christine, John said, "If you would be so kind, Major? One last moment of your time."

John held the tent flap open for her to enter and he followed her in, closing the flap behind them. They fell into each other's arms and let the grief of the loss and wounding of loved ones out in a rush of held-back emotions.

Outside, the corporal leaned over and spoke into the

major's ear. "Well, serving with women does have its advantages," he said with a leer.

"Corporal," said the RSM, having appeared unnoticed behind the pair of British troops, giving the man a cuff on the back of the head which knocked his cap off. "The general and his cousin the major have just been told that the general's sister has been killed in France and that the major's mother was wounded in the same raid. You had better get something straight right now and fast. The women in this regiment will cut your heart out and eat it in front of you before you even know you're dead if you so much as look at them the wrong way. The male troopers will do even worse. Do I make myself clear, Corporal? This is a front-line combat unit, not a rear-area playground. Now get that headgear on and your asses over to the practice range. Until you prove yourself to me and the rest of the regiment, you're both a pair of common recruits, worthy only of contempt and ridicule. Go on, get your asses out of my sight."

"Goddamn Brits," he said; then, looking at the departing truck carrying the German, "Goddamn Europeans."

Twenty minutes later, the cousins had recomposed themselves and exited the tent.

"John," Christine said. "Do you think it would be

possible for me to join the crew of a car?"

John motioned her to a seat at the table. "Have you thought this through, Chris?" he said. "Our men will accept you; they are used to seeing women fight and serving beside them. If you didn't mind being dirty and hungry, you would have stayed home. Being wounded or killed comes with being a soldier. But have you thought on what could happen if you are captured? That is what concerns me."

"Do you really think that wearing a nurse's uniform and serving in a hospital would save me from that if we were overrun John?" she said, putting her hand on his arm.

"No I suppose not," John said. "The fact that you are a field-grade officer with little practical experience may be a problem. I'll make you a deal: I'll put you in with an experienced crew and commander. When the commander tells me you can command your own car, then you'll do just that."

"Yes!" Christine said. "Just like a normal subby out for the first time. Until I get the hang of how things work."

"Right then," John said. "Lieutenant, is my vehicle ready? I want to see the commander and when I get back, I want a staff meeting, majors and above, all branches."

After meeting with the Commander of the Allied forces and informing him that he would begin moving in two days and that he wanted to hand over control of the prisoners that afternoon, John left the command tent and was headed to his vehicle when he was approached by two separate parties. The first was Major Lawrence, who was accompanied by an Arab dressed in rich flowing traditional garments.

"General Bekenbaum, it is my pleasure to introduce you to Feisal of the house Saud, the leader of the Saudi tribe," said Lawrence.

"A pleasure to meet you, my lord," said John. "Major Lawrence has told me much of you and your people."

"The pleasure is all mine, General," said Feisal. "My people have spoken of your great deeds, your heroism and your generosity. These are qualities my people value highly. My people have also been on the wrong side of your people in the past. You fight hard, then are gracious in victory. This also is admired by my people."

"My troopers will appreciate you saying so, my lord," John said. "After all, it is they who do all the work."

"Did I not tell you, Feisal?" said Lawrence. "He will not take all the credit, I said."

"And I did not believe you, it is true," Feisal replied. "All the British officers I have met take all the credit when things go well," he said to John, "but blame the men when things go wrong. No, General, if the men are not well led, they will not fight well. If the men do not trust and love their commander, they will not fight for him. I have watched your men. They remind me of my people. I thought maybe it was because of your machines that you are so good, but no. I see your people doing things on horseback that my people cannot do even with saddles. I see even your women are better warriors than most of my men. I see that they obey your every command no matter how big or how small without hesitation. This is the proof of a great leader. Thank you for coming to my country and helping us rid ourselves of the hated Turk." He bowed to John. "Your speech last night was inspiring. I had not thought a Christian would be so thoughtful."

"I have no religion," said John. "I find that it causes more problems than it solves. I am a believer, but not a follower. All the prophets are as one to me."

"Ah you see, Lawrence," said Feisal. "Another man like myself who does not let religion run his affairs but respects it just the same. The British tell me that your family knows about oil and petrol," he said to John. "They also tell me my land has much of this oil and that they would like to produce it after this nastiness is all over. Would you like to be a part of that as well?"

"My father has some oil, but we do not drill or look

for it," said John. "Others do that for us. Our company has developed and installed some small local refineries and upgrade facilities to pump oil. We have also designed and built some rail cars to transport the oil, which we lease to the railroads, and have designed and built some pipelines. When, as you say, this nastiness is over and if you are still interested, I am sure the Canadian consulate will provide you with a means to get in touch with us."

"Ah, Lawrence," said Feisal. "You see he is humble even in this. Unlike others."

"Well, my lord," said John. "I am not here to do business. I am here because my country asked me to fight our enemies here. Perhaps in the future, if I survive, we can speak of other things. I do not wish to be rude, but I must make preparations for another task."

Feisal and Lawrence made their goodbyes and John turned to the next delegation, this one of Turks, who addressed him in Russian.

"General, I would like to thank you for your memorial and your treatment of my men," the Turkish general said.

"I am sure you would do the same for us," John said.

"We would try, but our resources are sadly lacking," said the general. "Overhearing what you were saying to that rebel Arab, we in Turkey too could use some of your expertise. We have heard you modify those vehicles you use yourself. I am talking of the transports, not the fighting vehicles. We have a large country with little rail transport because of the terrain, but many roads. The ability to move goods and materials in vehicles like that would help tremendously. Also how you utilize radio equipment is novel. After this war is over and things return to normal, perhaps you could return and help us in these areas?"

"As I told the Arab earlier," John said. "My family's company has expertise in these areas. After all this is done and things become normal, I am sure if you contact the Canadian consulate, they will be able to get in contact with us. I am but a simple soldier and farmer. I am afraid I know little of these things."

"Just so," said the general. "As am I. But is not looking out for your country's growth and best interests also a part of being a soldier? Please remember this conversation; I do not believe my country will long be in this war. We are already negotiating an end to it with the new Russian government."

"Unfortunately, as long as my country is fighting the Germans, this will not end soon for me," said John. "I will inform my father of your offer after hostilities have stopped, not before. Now if you will excuse me, General, my time is limited."

Reaching his command tent John sat down and composed a message in the family's private code for his father, telling him of the conversations with the two leaders of the opposing groups. When he was done he passed it to a waiting messenger, telling him to send it with that night's report to home base.

In the regiment's tradition, staff meetings generally revolved around a meal, in this case dinner, and the smell of the cooking meal reminded John not only of the meeting, but that he had eaten little that day. One by one the commanders trickled in, the talk about normal life and tribulations in camp. Everyone had an easy manner with the others, and as soon as the last officer was seated, dinner was served, the conversation still light. The Indian colonel and major were sitting with the British major, and the female officers of the regiment were mixed in with the males, their laughter and jibes just as ribald as the males'.

Too soon the meal was over, and the officers lit pipes, cigars and cigarettes as glasses of vodka were poured and placed beside each officer. John rose and was followed by everyone else at the table.

"God save the King, our country and our regiment," he said, hoisting his glass. As one the regiment tossed back the fiery liquid and slammed the glasses onto the table, the British and Indian officers grimacing and coughing as their throats burned.

"You will find it never gets any better," John said, smiling, to the three officers trying to stifle coughs. "We just hide it better."

He waved at waiting aides, and they brought packages of papers to their officers, some larger than others.

"That is all the data and maps we have been able to obtain about the terrain and enemy forces we are likely to find in the area we must travel to get where we are going. It is a three-thousand-mile trip. High command would like us to hit any valuable targets of opportunity on the way, so instead of making at best one hundred fifty miles a day, we should plan on one hundred. So we are looking at thirty days' travel. Hopefully we will have good weather and some decent roads so we can average thirty miles an hour, but I don't think we should count on it.

"Congratulations to the newcomers to the regiment are in order. The Indian lancers, the good major there and his corporal, all passed minim standards – the Indians in particular almost all made Eagle status. Well done, gentlemen.

"Colonel Makarov, please work out a plan with Colonel Singh. I want his troops integrated with ours at first to learn the ropes. Once they have enough expertise, you can assign them their own cars. Will there be any problem with that, Colonel Singh?"

"No, sir," said the colonel. "Most of my people speak passable English and I will assign an English speaker with those who do not."

"Very well," said John. "Major Hood, you will be assigned a position in one of my personal guard cars, and I expect you to be at my side whenever we stop. You have much to learn, Major.

"Colonel Makarov, Major Bekenbaum has exercised her prerogative as an Eagle to join a line unit. Please assign her to one of the scout cars as with any new recruit. She is to be treated as such until she can demonstrate command abilities."

"General, that will leave me a major short on my nursing staff," said the male colonel of the medical staff.

"Promotion is a fact of life in the field, Colonel," said John. "I am sure you have a capable captain who can assume Major Bekenbaum's duties. While we are on the medical subject, you might as well report, Colonel."

"All the wounded are progressing well," said the colonel. "They should all be ready for transport home by the end of the month. The British have arranged transport through Panama and to Vancouver for them. They will also supply the medical staff to supervise during the transport. All medical supplies expended have been replaced and requested overages have been filled. We are as ready as we will ever be, General."

John received similar reports from the supply and services people, the artillery commander and the combat commanders. All was in readiness.

"First scouts out at daybreak," ordered John. "Main column a half hour later. After the first day we start looking for chances to do mayhem. Any questions?"

A few small issues were resolved quickly and the meeting was over.

As organized confusion took over, John took advantage of not having anything of his own to do for once and did nothing. Nothing but sleep.

Chapter Four

Two days later, the scout teams came back to camp at nightfall reporting targets for the first time: two towns situated ahead of them on a rail line, both with depots and barracks of Turks. The towns were ten miles apart, and John would hit them both. He ordered twenty-five armored cars to attack each town, fifteen cars for the barracks and ten for the depots. They were to approach in the darkness and hit the towns as daybreak occurred. The main column would continue on its path ready to support if any of the attacking groups got pinned down with the forty cars not needed for scouting.

    The attacking group set off at midnight and John tried vainly to go back to sleep after they had left. Daybreak and the main column set off once again, radio operators in the radio truck with earphones and radios on, waiting for any word from the raiding parties. Shortly after ten the radio truck sped up to drive parallel to John's, car and a message handed over. It was a simple and short message from the closest raiding group.

    MA NO MIA KIA PTR.

    Mission accomplished, no wounded or killed,

proceeding to rendezvous.

Looking over his left shoulder John could see a large black cloud of smoke rising from the direction of that town; further along a smaller column was appearing, turning blacker and thicker, and it wasn't long before the second attack group made the same report. So far so good, thought John.

Two weeks of the same followed. Sometimes they would hit towns with depots; sometimes they would hit towns with no depots. For days they would hit nothing, then hit everything. Anyone who could read a map could tell where they were going – they were following a straight line to their destination – but they were traveling too fast for the enemy to do anything but try and anticipate the next attack and set an ambush.

The sun was going down. Camp had been set up, sentries posted and maintenance done on vehicles. The troopers had been fed and camp had settled down, as the troopers sat in front of their tents or lounged on vehicle fenders and hoods, idly chatting. John was seated on one campstool, with his feet up on another. His field desk, a small flat surface with collapsible legs, was beside him. A tin cup of black coffee with a pot was sitting on it, and John had just lit a last cigar. He drank in the silence and looked at the open landscape around him. It was not much different than the prairies back home, but a little hotter and dryer. They would bypass the next town and hit the one after, before splitting away to the east and a hard nonstop run to Afghanistan. A light wind had sprung up and the temperature began to drop, so John shrugged on his tunic to hold the chill at bay.

"Excuse me, General," Colonel Makarov said. "These gentlemen have some important information you need to hear."

John looked up to see the colonel with three Arabs. Two were dressed in traditional clothing, while the third wore a British colonel's uniform with an Arab headdress. Both colonels had their right hands at the salute. John waved his right hand at his forehead and gestured to the men to sit down.

"Major Hood," he called out. "Four more cups and see if you can wrangle up some biscuits or something, will you? I am afraid the coffee is a bit weak for your tastes and the biscuits will be a little dry, but it is the best I can offer."

"No, no," the Arab colonel said. "Colonel Makarov was most generous and had us share a meal with him."

Hood appeared with cups in hand, his corporal behind him with a tray of biscuits and a small bowl of olive oil, which he placed on the small table. The corporal then touched up John's cup, before filling the other four. Then he and Hood took a few steps back and assumed the at ease position. John took a biscuit and dipped it in the olive oil and gestured the others to follow suit. After taking a sip and a bite of biscuit, the older Arab began to speak.

"This is the headman of the next town," the Arab colonel said, translating for his elder. "He thanks you for your hospitality and asks Allah to bless your wives with many sons, your herds of sheep and horses to cover the land in plenty and that your name be remembered forever."

"I thank him for his prayers," John said. "I wish the same for him. It is the custom of my people to have only one wife and we have herds of cattle not sheep."

The colonel translated his words and the other man nodded, then had a quick little laugh and said some more.

"He says having only one wife is foolish," the colonel said. "If you have only one wife, she will fight with you. If you have more than one, they fight with each other."

"I can see the wisdom in what he says," John said smiling. "I have not the pleasure of a wife as yet, so would not know these things. Unfortunately, our women would not tolerate what he says and a man could end up very dead very quickly."

"He agrees," the colonel said. "He has seen your

women with their weapons and they are very fierce looking. He has some daughters that are very beautiful and they would not be as fierce. Perhaps he can make some arrangement with you in this regard."

"I am sure his daughters would be most suitable," John said. "Unfortunately my mother would have to approve and she is the leader of the women warriors. So you see my problem."

The old man leaned back in his chair and took another sip of his coffee. Just then the breeze picked up and briefly billowed the regimental flag out fully. His eyes grew big and he quickly asked another question.

"He asks if your parents were with the people who fought in Afghanistan years ago," the colonel said.

"Yes," John said. "My father was the commander and my mother was his second in command."

"Then he thanks Allah that you are on our side," the colonel said. "Your mother shot his horse out from under him and only Allah's grace in providing him with another fast mount allowed him to survive. He says that with you on our side, we cannot but defeat those who stand against us. With your leave, he will return to his town and make ready."

With that said, the two Arabs rose and saluted John before quickly striding away.

"General," the Arab colonel said, "the Turks have unloaded a battalion of troops at his town. They intend on blocking your route and holding you until another two battalions come in tomorrow. This first battalion has two batteries of field guns and another two batteries of machine guns. They will be in place before you arrive tomorrow."

"Hood, bring the maps," John said. "Show me," he added as the map was spread out.

"Here, sir," the colonel said. "The road narrows between two hills and the Turks will block the exit. By the time you find your way around, the other troops will have unloaded and come up from behind you."

"Do you have the timetable of the trains and where they are going to unload?" John asked.

The colonel showed him on the map. There would be two trains a half hour apart and they would be unloaded at a siding behind which the ambush would take place.

"I can show you a way around," the colonel said. "It will bypass the ambush and not put you behind schedule very much."

John looked at the map for a few minutes and lit another cigar before leaning back in his chair and smiling.

"I think not, Colonel," John said. "I think not. Makarov, staff meeting now! Hood, another pot of coffee for the colonel here, and a jug for me."

"Would that be this vodka I hear about, General?" the Arab colonel asked. "I have heard this is better than that awful scotch the British give us."

Once all the staff had assembled, John laid out his plan. All but four of the scout cars would leave immediately for the ambush site. They were to find a way to the east of the site around to the rear, and find positions on each side of the road on the hilltops and in the front for the field guns and armored cars. Two hours before dawn, all of the Eagles and the field guns would head for the ambush site. Five hundred troops and the field guns would proceed to contact right up the road, five hundred more to each side and the last five hundred to curve around the rear. The field guns' task was to eliminate the enemy field batteries, then the machine gun positions. The armored cars would form defensive postures and use their heavy machine guns to engage the enemy machine guns and the Lewis guns to engage the infantry. The frontal force's task was to hold the enemy's attention. Once the flankers were in position on the sides, they were to engage anything and everything. The rear force was to hold the enemy from escaping. Three quarters of the medical staff were to accompany the Eagles and set up to the rear of the field guns.

The Bears would also leave two hours before daybreak. They would split into two equal forces. A mile before the enemy would stop at a siding to unload, the rail line had a series of curves that led to and from a two-hundred-yard-long bridge across a steep gorge. The first group of Bears would head to the curve leading away from the bridge and remove all of the outside spikes holding the rails to the ties on four sections of rail, starting just after the apex of the corner. They would also remove plates holding the four sections of rails together. As the train passed over this section of track, centrifugal force would force the rails apart and the inside trucks should come off the inside rail, causing the train to wreck. Once the train came to a stop, every gun would fire into the cars and anything that moved in or outside of them.

Once the first train had passed, the second group of Bears were to do the same thing to the set of rails leading into the bridge and both rails of the bridge itself. Hopefully, the train would wreck on the bridge itself. Once the last car of the second train had entered the curve, the telegraph line was to be cut. All of the telegraph poles were to be set on fire and the bridge was to be destroyed. Once the train and the bridge were destroyed, they would head to the first train and link up with the first group of Bears and then proceed to the rear of the ambush sight.

No prisoners were to be taken and the enemy was to be left to handle their own casualties.

"Excuse me, General," the Arab colonel said. "My people have been derailing trains for some time now. The Turks have become cautious. If they see a rail missing, they immediately stop and reverse, or in this case, they will unload the troops and assault any likely ambush sights. In any case, they will replace the rails and be on their way in a short time."

"If we were going to remove the rails, I would agree, Colonel," John said. "But we are not. We are only removing the spikes and holding plates. To the engineer, the rails will look perfectly fine until they split apart. Then he will jam on the brakes, which will cause the rails to spread further, and soon the cars will be on the ground."

"General, they have also pulled all of their garrison troops from the surrounding towns and placed them in the next town," the Arab colonel said. "There are about five hundred of them. They have a train for them and once they receive word from the ambush site, that train will leave to provide reinforcements."

"Well then, Colonel," John said. "It would be a great help if you and your men could help us by taking out that train for us. And look at all of the opportunities you will have with all of the unguarded towns afterward."

"Not to mention all of the weapons and ammunition the train will have on it," the colonel said. "We can use them badly."

"You can have anything you can grab from all of the trains," John said. "We will not have time to salvage any of it ourselves. OK, if there are no further questions? Everyone to his task."

An hour and a half after daybreak, the first Bear ambush had been set up. The rails had been sabotaged and the telegraph line had been spliced into and was being monitored. John and his command group were with this group of Bears and he had set up so that he could observe the action. The Eagles had surprised the Turks at the blocking site and if John had not received radio transmission telling him, he could hear the field guns, which would have let him know the eagles were in action in any case. The Turks had telegraphed the information that the attack was early and the trains were on their way a half hour apart and coming fast.

The second ambush site radioed that the first train was entering their position, and the first ambush made ready. Soon they could see the smoke rising from the locomotive as it accelerated around the curve; this was followed by the sound of the drive wheels and pistons. The train was coming hard and fast. As it came into view, you could tell the Arab train attacks had had an effect on the Turks. In front of the locomotive was a flat car with sandbagged positions on it. It was armed with a machine gun and two rifle teams. The locomotive itself had armor protecting the vulnerable parts and another manned flatcar right behind it with still another behind the passenger cars and stockcars, carrying a battery of field guns.

True to plan, the second unspiked rail section began to spread as the locomotive hit it. The engineer, sensing something was wrong, jammed on the brakes and rammed the engine into reverse, causing sparks to fly from the rails and drive wheels, but it was far too late as the leading car and then the locomotive hit the ground and the rails split right apart. Then the armored transports of the Bears roared into view, turning sideways and letting loose with every Vickers and Lewis gun they had, while the concealed dismounted troopers fired into the cars. The crash itself was spectacular. The locomotive fell on its side and the boiler ruptured, sending scalding steam into the leading flatcar. The following flatcar, being lighter than the passenger cars following, was thrust upward, spilling the troops. Several of the first passenger cars also were thrust upward as the weight of the cars behind pushed them. Rail trucks and wheels, no longer having weight holding them to the tracks, flew in every direction. Cars were crumpled and crushed: some tipped up, but most fell on their sides. Sparks were flying everywhere and glass was breaking, not only from the impact of the ground, but from the bullets hitting it. Screams of wounded men and horses reverberated through the countryside, and soon the Bears stopped firing into the cars.

    A few shots rang out as foolish troopers tried to engage the Canadians after escaping the carnage of the train, but this too came to an end, and the Turks started to try and help their wounded. The Canadians, though appalled at the carnage, followed their orders and just observed.

    Twenty minutes later, the crash of the second train was heard, and the firing there was also short. John then ordered the telegraph poles at his location to be set on fire and more smoke could be seen coming from the second ambush site too. Ten minutes later a plume of dust and truck engine noises could be heard and John ordered his group to mount up.

    The second column of the Bears passed through at full speed, headed for the rear of the Eagles, and their commander pulled his vehicle alongside John's.

    "Jesus, what a mess," he said. "Our train went right

off the bridge and into the gorge. We didn't even use much more than one clip each of ammunition. The locomotive set the bridge on fire itself. We had to scramble just to get across ourselves before it was fully engulfed. We have zero casualties, sir."

"Very well, Colonel," John said. "Join your group. We are right behind you."

By the time John reached the Eagles' positions, the fighting was over. As soon as the Turks saw the first of the Bear vehicles coming and deploying to their rear, with another group right behind, they surrendered. Eagles were cautiously coming down from their positions on the hills and medics were gathering the wounded and taking them to the medical tents at the rear.

The enemy field artillery had been hit hard. Bodies were strewn all around the guns, some of which were smoking and a few with barrels lying beside broken trucks and wheels. Many of their infantry were lying in rows, which told John the machine guns had done deadly work. No trenches had been dug or defense works prepared, in fact, many of the dead and wounded were lying in front of or on top of their tents, some of which were burning. Four armored cars and a hundred Eagle troopers with bayonets fixed were watching the enemy stack rifles in neat piles, while others guarded other enemy troops collecting the rifles from the fallen. Still more enemy troops were gathering their wounded, and surgeons were beginning their trade. Dead and wounded horses, some still attached to their horse lines, littered the area, and shots were ringing out as John's troops moved about the field putting the wounded beasts out of their misery. Many of the troopers doing this had tears in their eyes.

The Bear, medical and Eagle colonels came up to his command vehicle and John stepped down.

"What's the damage, Colonel?" John asked the medical officer.

"Thirty lightly wounded, sir," the man said. "Most of them minor scrapes or shrapnel wounds from ricochets. I will have my people start helping the enemy now, sir."

"No time for that," John said. "Get our wounded and your gear loaded. I want us out of here in no more than an hour. Colonel," he said, addressing the Bears' commander, "see if you can salvage any of those field guns. Load up all of the captured small arms and machine guns and all of the ammunition we can carry.

"Report, Colonel Makarov."

"We caught them napping, General," Makarov said. "Most of them were still asleep, and we just fired into the tent lines. The Germans tried to engage: those are the ones you see lying in rows. We wiped out the crews as they were trying to man the guns. It was pretty much over by the time you fellows showed up. Other than a few dents and missing paint, we have no damage, sir."

"Get the scouts out right now," John said. "Tell them to follow the road by the tracks for about ten miles. Then take the next road heading east and look for a decent camp area about a half hour after that. Have the rest of the Eagles help the Bears loading the weapons and ammunition. Like I said, I want to be on the move in less than an hour. Hood! Escort our guests over here."

"Well, Colonel, this is becoming a habit," John said in German. The German colonel he had let go from their first engagement was approaching. This time he was weaponless and hatless, and had a bandage wrapped around his head. "I trust your wound is not serious?"

The German colonel just bowed his head in salute and had a little grin on his face.

"Oh, you are expecting reinforcements?" John said, then pointed to the columns of smoke now visible from the train wrecks. "Unfortunately, I am afraid they will be very late. We greeted them before we came here and oh yes, it looks like our allies have taken care of the train coming from the north as well."

A column of black smoke, growing larger, could be seen over the northern horizon and the smiles disappeared.

"We were not expecting you until tomorrow," the German said. "Things would have been different then."

"Should have, could have, would have," John said. "Like my mother taught me, hope for the best, prepare for the worst."

"We can expect some help from your medical people?" the German asked.

"No, I am afraid not," John said. "First, I have no time. Second, even if I had the time I would not. Tell your superiors, that the next time they bomb and kill Canadian medical people, we won't even leave any wounded behind. Reap what you sow, Colonel, reap what you sow.

"Come on, get the show on the road!" he yelled, walking away from the stunned German and Turkish commanders. "We don't have all bloody day!"

"What did he mean by that?" the German asked Major Hood, who, not speaking German, had to have it translated.

"It seems your chaps in France air bombed a clearly marked Canadian hospital located way behind the lines," Hood said. "The attack killed and wounded a number of medical people and killed more of the wounded soldiers, and the hospital burned to the ground. The general's aunt and a cousin were wounded and his sister killed. All of them nurses. I think he is showing a tremendous amount of restraint. I would have just killed all of you."

That night, John had a staff meeting with all of the officers over the rank of major. "Right then," he said. "Secondary task complete. Tomorrow we head northeast away from the rail line to our primary objective. The Huns and Turks will be scrambling all over looking and preparing for attacks that will never come. Our Indian friends are doing well in their own cars, Major Hood here is getting a sense of humor, all is right with the world."

"Don't have a bloody choice, do I?" said Hood. "Someone has to keep you bloody colonials in line. Why the world would come to an end without a member of His Majesty's Army to keep you all properly focused."

"Bloody hell," said Singh. "I bet you don't even know where you are right now."

"Why, certainly I do," said Hood. "I am sitting at the general's table somewhere between Never Been There and Haven't Got a Clue."

After the laughter had settled down, the Brit and the Indian traded turns at being the straight man and mimicking each other's accents and mannerisms, exaggerating each, and then John started the briefing in earnest.

Chapter Five

Ten days later, the four hundred vehicles pulled into Kandahar, townspeople watching warily as they climbed a nearby hill and began setting up camp in what they found out later had been his father's camp years before. Some of the townsmen came and watched them form their laagers and guard posts, noting the Union Jack on the red field of the national colors. This elicited some comments, as did the turbaned Indian troops. All movement stopped when the regiment's standard was raised, and many of the men started to point and chatter and some pelted back into the town. Soon nervous guards were watching as the field between the town and the camp began to fill with people, many of them armed. John stood watching the crowd, trying to gauge their mood, especially the armed ones who looked tough, with scowls on their faces.

  The RSM appeared walking toward him with a Lewis gun, magazine mounted on top, in his hands. He tossed it at a surprised John, who caught it deftly, then the RSM grabbed the regimental colors, jerking them out of the ground, motioned John to follow him and jumped onto the hood of the armored car closest to the crowd. As John mounted it to stand next to him, the RSM pointed at the crowd.

"Jack a round and put the gun on your hip, barrel up, fire three rounds rapid, then yell 'Kandahar we have returned!' at the top of your lungs in Russian, then empty the magazine," said the RSM. "Do it now."

Not asking any questions, John fired the three rounds and yelled the words as the RSM began to swirl the colors around his head. Almost immediately the armed men yelled out and fired their rifles in the air, dancing with glee as John let loose with the Lewis on full automatic until it was empty. To the people of the town, the regiment had come home.

For the first night in a month, John slept through the night, not woken up by a question or tossing and turning worried about a raid in progress. He woke midmorning hungry but refreshed and walked out of the tent, blinking at the light.

"Breakfast, my lord?" asked a strangely accented Russian female voice. John discovered he now had several servants to look after his needs.

"They hauled me over here this morning too," Christine said from a chair at the table.

"Not good Lady Bekenbaum spend time away from family," an older male servant said, and the RSM too was escorted to the table by several other older males.

As they finished their meal, Major Hood approached, escorting an old Catholic priest in a frayed black cassack.

"This is Father Paul, general," said Major Hood. "He has come to ask permission to say mass for the men, sir."

"So," said John. "Do I call you Uncle Paul or Father Bekenbaum?"

"Right now, my son, it is Father Bekenbaum," said his father's older brother. "I am led to believe you have not celebrated mass for some time now. I would celebrate the sacraments with your troops."

"By all means, Father," John replied. "You may celebrate mass for those who wish it."

"Thank you, General," said the priest. "Now, nephew, get me some vodka and tell me of your life and that of your father and lovely mother.

"Brother-in-law Wilhelm, you are looking your age," the priest continued.

"Father Paul, so good of you to notice," replied the RSM. "You are looking far older than yours."

"Christine, I present your father's uncle, Father Paul Bekenbaum," said John. "Father Paul, your niece, Johannes's youngest daughter, Christine."

The four spent until the sun was heading over the horizon learning about each other and their lives, at times laughing, others crying, and by the end of the evening all were happy.

Mass was held the next morning and John took the opportunity to go for a walk. It had been arranged that those who, like himself, did not want to partake, would post guard while the others went to mass. Even so, about a quarter of the troops were relaxing or doing repairs to camp or equipment. John came to a clearing and observed the Indian troopers, shirts off, going through motions with swords that at times looked like an intricate display of ballet, and it reminded him that since he left home he had not done any of his own training. John moved off some distance, removed his boots and socks, hat and pistol belt, took off his uniform jacket and tie and unbuttoned several buttons on his shirt. Rolling up his pant legs to just under his calves, he started the first slow easy movements of his Tai Chi regimen and was soon joined by his entourage of aides and bodyguards. Two guards stayed alert, not taking part, as the area was still unknown to them and dangers could be anywhere.

    Word soon got out and the little group was joined by everyone in camp who wasn't on guard duty or at mass. The sight of over a thousand men and women in lines, perfectly executing the slow intricate hand and leg movements in unison, not a word of command spoken, was impressive to behold. For over an hour they exercised, and by the end John had worked up a sweat and muscles unused for several months were beginning to complain. Looking around, he saw they had been watched by the Indians and a large group of Afghan men.

Colonel Singh approached John as he was lacing up his boots, waited until he had finished, then saluted. "I saw those moves demonstrated when I served in Hong Kong," he said. "But never in such a large group. It looks impressive, but I don't see how slow moves like that would be helpful in a real battle."

"The muscles and the brain will remember what needs to be done," replied John. "These exercises are to train the muscles and relax the mind. I noticed your people have a similar routine, although much faster: do I hear a challenge being issued?"

"One of mine against one of yours?" said the Colonel.

Each called one of his men over and explained. The combatants would use their own training and the competition would end when the first man hit the ground. The Indian was a very tall and well-built man, over two hundred pounds, while John's man was tall and slim, giving up twenty or thirty pounds to the Indian. The Indian circled the Canadian, who stood calmly shifting his feet slowly to keep the Indian in view. Suddenly, in a blur of motion, the Indian attacked, throwing an overhand punch with his left hand, while going for an encirclement move with his right arm. Stepping out of the reach of the Indian's right arm, the Canadian absorbed the punch with his right hand clasping over the Indian's fist, twisted and, with a flick of his wrist, used the larger man's weight and energy back over the left leg he had extended behind him, so that the Indian found himself looking up from the ground on his back. Taking two steps back, the Canadian grasped his right fist with his left palm, holding them on his chest and bowed to his opponent, turned and left the field.

John walked over to the fallen man, extending his hand to help him to his feet.

"You lasted longer than I did," John said, patting the soldier on the back. Looking over the man's shoulder he saw prim khaki-uniformed, white pith-helmeted heads coming their way. "Looks like the holiday is over," he said to Singh.

"We have been here what, all of two days?" the Indian colonel said.

"If you couldn't take a joke, you shouldn't have joined," John repeated the old joke, then turned to greet the arrivals. "How can I help you, Captain?" he asked the British officer returning his salute.

"We have entered into negotiations with the Turks on a ceasefire agreement and you are to halt all offensive movements against them," the captain answered. "You are to prepare your regiment for redeployment to the Western Front and I am to tell the consulate when you will be ready to move."

"I see," said John. "Well, Captain, you can tell the consulate that I will give them my plans as soon as I find out where I have to go and what supplies I will require for that move."

Dismissing the earnest Brit, John called over his officer of the day. "Send a message to the raiding parties to return to base," he ordered. "No offensive actions, though they may defend themselves if required. The same for the patrols starting now. Have my staff assemble for dinner this evening and tell them to prepare for movement orders.

"Well, Colonel," he said to the Indian. "It appears they want us in the big show. I will try and find a way out of it for your men if you want."

"Thank you, sir," replied the colonel. "I have learned some things from you during our time together, I will discuss it with my men and give you an answer at the meeting."

Next, a group of well-dressed Afghans came forward, escorted by Father Bekenbaum. The group arranged themselves in a line and saluted in the British fashion.

"Sir," a man of about John's father's age said in British-accented English. "I had the pleasure of assisting your mother and father in that great battle many years ago. I am the leader of my people and we have moved our settlement to that location. We have taken all of the advice your great father gave us and, like he foresaw, we have become prosperous. We would count it a great honor if you and your mighty warriors would bless us with a visit."

"How far away is it?" John asked. "Unfortunately the British have cut short our stay and we have to leave soon."

"It is but six hours' easy ride from here," the man said. "To the west on the road to Iran."

"Well then, sir," John said. "You can expect us two hours after dawn in two days' time, as that is the road we have to take to our new destination."

They exchanged greetings and the men left and John headed to his quarters.

Outside his tent, John accepted a cup of coffee from a servant and, plopping the big file of papers on the table, began to read. The more he read, the more disturbed he became. The officer of the day returned and John ordered a radio connection to home base as soon as could be arranged, then wrote out the message he wanted to send and handed it to the lieutenant. He continued reading the papers and started making talking points and preliminary plan outlines for what he wanted to do. All too quickly the day passed. He received an answer from his father back at base, in which Andreas agreed to his plan, and, putting the papers back in the file, went into his tent to dress for the staff meeting.

"We have been out of touch for some time," John began the meeting after the last of the dinner dishes had been removed. "To bring you up to speed, the big German offensive that started in March petered out in July. Our friends the ANZACs seem to have learned from us, and have been hammering the Huns from behind in small but devastating raids, setting up what our commanders feel will be the final devastating attack that will end this war."

John then went on to outline that high command wanted their expertise in mobile motorized small-unit warfare and, as a result, they would be transferring to the Western Front. A ceasefire and safe conduct had been arranged so that the regiment could transit from Afghanistan directly to a port on the Black Sea on the Iranian coast. It was a trip of just over two thousand miles, but the roads were supposed to be in good shape and they should be able to average two hundred miles per day.

In addition, British high command had requested a

special mission to evacuate Russian aristocrats who were located in Odessa. The regiment had been requested because of its ties to the region and familiarity with the area. A four-company, or half-battalion, force was requested for this mission, and sea transport would be provided for troops and one hundred vehicles.

John listened as the officers voiced concern for relatives and friends in the settlements their fathers had left, and said how unjust it was for the rich and well connected to get out but not the regular people.

"The earl and countess are also concerned," John said. "The earl has demanded and received permission to evacuate as many as wish to come. He estimates five thousand people all told, but that many families will not wish to leave. We have permission to evacuate five thousand, no more. The situation in Russia is chaotic. Bolsheviks and loyalists are actively fighting a civil war and the situation is constantly changing. At the moment the area is controlled by the loyalists, or Whites, but the Bolsheviks are reported to be making plans for a big offensive there, so things may change by the time we arrive. Food and supplies are scarce and I feel we must be prepared for anything. Therefore I am amending the orders and we will be sending one thousand troopers and one hundred vehicles on that operation, forty of which I want to be armored cars."

"What's the timeframe" Colonel Makarov asked.

"They want us on the front line in France no later than the middle of October. We will leave here tomorrow morning. We have been invited by a tribe who fought with my father here to view the original battlefield and to participate in a feast. I think it important we do so. It should take us no more than two hours to reach the town site and another hour to set up camp. We should expect to stay two days. After that we will head for the embarkation port.

"Colonel Makarov will oversee and accompany the transport of three thousand troopers and their vehicles to France, where he will be met by my brother Stephan, who will take over temporary command. In no way are you to undertake any offensive actions beyond training and familiarization until I arrive with the remainder of the regiment. Is that clear?"

After a quick question-and-answer period, the meeting broke up, officers except for Majors Hood and Bekenbaum leaving to inform their personal staffs and to make plans for the moving of the troops.

After filling the two majors' glasses with some local brandy, John sat and poured himself a tall glass of the alcohol.

"Well, Alex, back to France eh?" John said.

"Not for me, sir," replied Alex. "Never been to France. Served as a staff officer in England then was transferred to the same post in Egypt. I think my family pulled some strings to keep me out of the fighting. I kept applying for a transfer to a front-line unit, but was refused."

"Well, I still need a liaison officer, so you're stuck with us, and now you will be coming with us to Odessa, before you get your chance to get killed in France," John said. "Not to worry, from the sounds of it, we are likely going to have many opportunities to die in Russia too."

"At least I will have the opportunity to see where Father came from," said Christine.

"Well, there is that," agreed John.

At that point Father Paul joined the threesome at the table, sitting down and helping himself to a large glass of brandy. "Is it true that the tsar has abdicated and that the country is at war with itself?" he asked.

"The only thing that everyone is agreed on," said John, "is that the Romanovs and all the old aristocratic families must go. The tsar and his family have been placed under house arrest. That is all I know."

"I would join you when you leave to evacuate the families," said Paul.

"They will be going to Canada, Uncle," said Christine.

"As will I," said the priest. "It is time I reunited with my family. There are younger priests here who can take my place." He slammed his empty glass on the table, stood and left.

"OK, mark him down as the regiments' chaplain so he is on the unit strength and not counted as a civilian," John ordered his officer of the day.

Chapter Six

The next morning, the regiment left Kandahar. The town's people lined the streets waving and cheering. As each vehicle reached the open road they accelerated to best speed. The road was good and they could average a good pace and reached the new town two hours later, as had been expected.

Unlike most other areas, the farms had little if any poppy growing. The fields were green and well tended. Farmyards and buildings were in good repair, unlike the rest of the country. The people looked well fed, their clothing colorful. While the women kept their hair covered by scarves, their faces were clear and they looked happy, heads held high instead of down, many of them waving and calling out as the troopers drove by.

They soon came to the town proper; the scouts had picked out a bivouac area for them and the vehicles pulled in and formed their laagers. These were not unlike the circling of the wagons from frontier days. The vehicles parked in a large circle, radio and command vehicles to the center along with the fuel and food trucks. Each vehicle was parked sideways in the circle and overlapping fields of fire from each vehicle were established. One trooper from each vehicle manned a Lewis gun and sentries were posted several yards in front of the laagers. Tents were being erected: one laager had the medical tent in the middle and another the command center.

The town itself was hidden from view by a wall thirty feet high. Nothing but well-kept lawns and gardens grew within two hundred yards of it. On each corner of the wall was a tower, as well as two towers bordering the front and rear gates. Field guns mounted on each tower boomed out a single shot in sequence as a salute when the national and regimental colors were raised in the command laager. At the front gate, an original version of the regimental flag, showing just the bear and eagle, rose on the right tower. The battlements and front towers were lined with cheering people.

Small ten-acre farms ringed the town, the homesteads well built and kept. Yards and gardens were neat and tidy, with many ornamental and fruit trees providing color and shade. Almost all of the homes had a paddock with four or five horses in them.

"Those ponies look familiar?" John asked Christine as she approached.

"They look a lot like ours back home," she said. "A little smaller though."

"Ya, I thought so too," John said. "Anybody seen the RSM?" he yelled. The RSM was usually the first one by his side when they stopped.

"Ya," said a trooper sitting in the top turret of one of the armored cars, pointing to an open pasture. "Him and a couple of other old timers are out there."

John and Christine clambered up to the top of the vehicle and John picked up his binoculars and scanned the area. Four older members of the regiment were striding out to the pasture. They were heading down a slight slope. On the left and right were grass-covered hills, a large hill rose about a mile beyond them and a road ran down the middle of it to the town at their rear. The four veterans stopped about three hundred yards from the town and stood in a line across the road for a moment. Then two walked to the right hill and one to the left. The RSM stood in the center of the road for a minute and then slowly walked to the left and slightly to the rear. He stopped and looked around, then his foot scrubbed on the ground and he squatted down; John focused the binoculars on him and saw him pick something up from the ground.

"Come on," John said. "Everybody, come on. You too, Hood."

The whole command group followed John and

Christine. John pulled the regimental colors from the rear fender of his command car and handed it to the nearest trooper, then he started for the field. Soon every trooper, except those on guard, had left the camp and followed. They walked in silence, only their boots on the road making any sound. Soon groups broke off, some to the right, some to the left hills. Bears and Eagles mixed in all three groups. John stopped behind the still-squatting RSM, the ones who had followed spread out behind him. No one spoke and everyone was looking around. It was a perfect killing field.

John stepped on something small and hard, and bent down to pick it up. It was a spent .44-caliber shell casing. The RSM stood and put a shell casing in his pocket. He began to speak, his voice shaking and low. He gestured around the area as he spoke.

"We were lined up across this road in two lines of five hundred," he said. "The colonel had scrounged every red jacket he could find from the Brits. Mine was way too small. The sleeves came to just below my elbows, I couldn't close it and I split the shoulder seams when I put it on. The Germans were five hundred yards to the front on our right, the Brits on our left, lined up in skirmish order. The Brits were wearing their light-colored work jackets. We wanted the bad guys to think they were us. Their horses were about fifty yards behind them. Ours were behind those hills to your right and left. The flag was behind us, planted in the ground, but furled so the bad guys could not see it."

He paused then, his hands on his hips, looking around. John saw that the groups to each side were similarly standing around the veterans on both hills, who were also gesturing, pointing the layout.

"We could feel them before we could see them," the RSM said. "The ground was vibrating and I knew there was a large group coming. First a few scouts crested the hill and stopped. Then a large group with banners came up. A man in the center of the banners gestured forward and they swarmed up over the hill. On and on they came, forming up in a solid block, five hundred wide. They planned just to bull right through us. God, the hill was a solid mass of horses and men, chanting, yelling, swirling swords around their heads, the front ranks punching lances in the air."

"They started to trot and the ground started to tremble: even at that distance the sound of the hooves was like thunder. The Brits started to sing, as did the Germans, though we could hardly hear the words. They fired two volleys each, then sprinted back for their horses. A couple fell, troopers galloped back to get them, but some were ridden over. The enemy came to a canter as the Brits and the

Germans joined our lines."

"'Beautiful day,' the colonel said as he rode in front of us. My knees were knocking and my hands were shaking. 'Easy pickings, boys, just aim at the group, you can't miss. Remember your training: aim and shoot, aim and shoot.'"

"Then he rode to the back and he lit a cigar. He started to hum and let the flag loose. We were at ease at that point and he called us to attention. The ground was vibrating so hard I couldn't tell if my knees were knocking or not. The colonel started to sing softly and we joined him. Christ I was scared." The RSM stopped speaking then. He was standing at attention, gripping an unseen rifle and staring to his front.

Then he abruptly turned sideways and brought his arms up like he was about to fire. He jacked his right hand down and back up, then reached to his chest, plucking an imaginary cartridge from a chest loop and loaded it.

"Present," he said quietly. "The bad guys were three hundred yards in front of us. Front rank five-round rapid fire, *fire!*" The RSM stood not moving his arms still holding the rifle. "Rear rank rapid fire, fire at will, *fire!*"

Then the RSM began the motions of firing a Winchester rifle over and over again.

"They came to a gallop after the first shots rang out, leveling lances. We shot and shot, stacking them up like cordwood. They tried to climb the fallen, but soon the barricade was too high and they started to fan out to try and flank us."

The RSM then gestured to the hills on both sides.

"That's when the Bears opened up on them. We were shooting three or four thousand rounds every couple of seconds into their massed ranks. We couldn't miss and they couldn't move. We slaughtered them like sheep."

The RSM became quiet again, his hands dropped to his sides, visibly shaking.

"They broke then, those that were left," he said. "We kept shooting. My barrel was so hot it glowed and the wood of the stock was smoking, burning my palm. I was almost deaf from the shots, my right shoulder was sore, my right cheek scorched, my right wrist and trigger finger sore. The flesh on my thumb and fingers raw from loading. Without orders we stopped shooting. The enemy was on the run and the tribesmen were hitting them hard as they ran, as did the Bears on the flanks."

He squatted down, his arms on his knees and head on his arms as he remembered. Then he stood and looked to his right and to his left and smiled. He gestured out and around him. "This is where we were born!" he yelled out, and he grabbed the colors from the trooper holding them and swirled them around. "This is where your mothers and fathers became Bears and Eagles!"

Then a voice to the rear began to sing and before the first verse was finished the group on the valley floor joined in. Not the original song, but the regiment's version of it. The valley vibrated as the massed voices from both hillsides joined in, and John walked up to the RSM, who had planted the flag in the ground and stood his hands on his hips, head held high and tears running down his cheeks. John put his arm around the man and held him close. Both men stood, tears staining the ground, as the regiment sang all around them.

The song finished and the valley came back to silence, birds started to sing again and the wind could be heard rustling through the tall grass. Then troopers began to move about the field, telling each other where their parents or relatives had stood, reliving the stories they had heard their whole lives. Some stooped and picked up old tarnished cartridge cases, then they started fanning out across the fields. The descendants of the German troopers showed where their ancestors had first lined up and pointed at the still visible bone fragments littered all over the field, most heavily one hundred yards in front of the main line.

Christine, John and the RSM quietly left them to the

field and returned to the camp, all of the guards coming to attention and saluting not John, but the RSM.

Reaching his tent, John motioned Christine and the RSM to sit and he went into the tent and came back with a bottle of rye whisky and three glasses, pouring a generous portion in each.

"The regiment," John said and the three shot back the amber liquid, then John filled them again. "The RSM," he said, holding his glass to the man and shooting it back. Then he sat.

Several Afghans approached with trays of food and placed them before the three.

"Eat first then go," said the older servant.

"I should have studied my Russian better," said Christine. "I am having trouble understanding these people."

"So are we," said John.

"OK, eat finish, now come," said the older gentlemen when they'd filled their stomachs.

They were taken a short way away and the RSM began to shake as they reached three well-kept and cared for graves. He fell to his knees, making the sign of the cross, tears running down his cheeks. Not fully understanding what was going on, John read the names written in Russian on the granite stone markers. What he read on the center stone made him pause and look at Christine for a moment, knowing she could not read what was written there.

"Hello Aunt Irene," John said in German and watched Christine as she understood what was going on. "I am your nephew John, I am your brother-in-law Andreas's youngest son, and I was born in a country called Canada. This young lady is Johannes's youngest daughter, Christine. Your daughter Susan is doing well and has a son and daughter of her own now. You must know that Uncle John waited a very long time, devoting his whole life to the regiment and to Susan, so much so that he almost killed himself. Aunt Wilhelmina came into our lives alone and lost and Mother brought the two of them together and saved both their lives. Willy is a good woman, and you would like her, Aunt Irene."

From his knees, the RSM struggled to his feet and with a low growl put his head back and shook it, getting control of his emotions.

"Sister, it is I, Wilhelm," he said. "Your daughter Susan grew up to be a beauty and she has the wit and humor of Yonny. She is strong and is now heading the nursing corps of the whole country's army."

Turning to the left headstone: "Jacob, you took an uncoordinated, nervous kid and made him a man. The lessons you taught me have saved my life more than once. Now I train other young uncoordinated nervous boys and teach them the lessons you have taught me. Thank you to both of you for making me the man I am."

"Leo," said Christine to the stone on the right. "Your family has never wanted. They live well with us in Canada and your grandson is an officer and in charge of a squadron. Irene, Mother, you are held up as an example to all the girls: your courage in the operating room and on the battlefield is what inspired me to try harder and to be the first woman to join the Eagles. To all three of you, thank you. Without you, none of us would be here today or living the wonderful life we live in Canada. Know that your names are not forgotten, know that your lives are celebrated.

"Mother, thank you for allowing me to experience the love of your man, my father, who all of us love and are loved by in return. Susan is my big sister and my mentor and my tormenter. We love each other more than life itself at times. Thank you."

The tears were now flowing unrestrained from her eyes and she clutched the RSM, who she had not known was her step uncle. John motioned for the retainers to join him and leave the couple to mourn and to learn about each other alone.

John came back to his now very quiet camp, sitting

down once again at his chair and pouring himself another shot of rye. All of his troops were still wandering about the old battlefield. The Indian colonel and Major Hood trailed by his corporal approached and John motioned them to sit and motioned to the bottle. "Corporal," he said. "If you would be so good? Grab another three glasses for us? There is another bottle on the bed. If you wouldn't mind giving the sentries and yourself a shot?"

John topped his glass up after filling the other two officers' glasses.

"That was you who fought here?" the Indian asked. "My father was in the relief force, but he said they were Russians."

"We were then," John said. "We came to Canada the next year."

"My father said the bodies were stacked four feet high at the front two or three ranks," the Indian said. "You could walk for yards without touching the ground. The dead stretched for a mile or more. My God. Your RSM spoke in Russian, but I understand enough to know what he was saying. He was here, yes?"

"Yes," John answered. "As were most of the mothers and fathers of my troops, or their uncles and aunts. So was he." He nodded at an older gentleman approaching them, dressed in a grey Russian type colonel's uniform and a light blue turban.

"Some tea, sir?" John asked in English.

"Colonel Ahkmed Sing Bashir at your service, General," the man said, saluting. John answered with a vague wave of his hand to his forehead. "I was hoping for some of your wonderful vodka," the man said.

"Sorry," John said, motioning to an empty chair and pouring some rye into an empty glass. "This is called rye whisky and comes from my country. I only have a few bottles and it is for special occasions."

Before the colonel could sit, the Indian had risen and began addressing the man in his own language. He bowed his head and made a gesture with his right hand that started at his heart and ended at his lips, and went to a knee. The colonel put both his hands on the Indian's shoulders and, raising him, kissed him on both cheeks, addressing him in the same language. Then he sat, saluted those at the table and shot the amber liquid back.

"That is not so fiery as your famous vodka," the colonel said after a grimace. "But very nice for all that. I should explain. The colonel and I," he said nodding to the Indian, "are not Muslim. Our teachings are much the same as what you believe. We were Muslims when your father came here, but we changed."

"The raj is much respected among my people," the Indian said. "Many of our holy men come here to hear him speak."

"Ach," Bashir said. "I merely repeat what this man's father taught me. I am as much a raj as Andreas is an earl. My people, like his did him, chose me to be their leader. I am just a man doing his best, as God wishes us all to do."

"Your people have prospered," John said.

"Following your father's suggestions, yes we have," Bashir said. "Our crops and herds do well and we produce more than we can consume and sell the excess. We plant about a tenth of our fields in poppy for a cash crop. As your father suggested, we charge ten percent of everything for tax. This we use to fund our schools and a small hospital. We send our brightest students to Kiev for higher learning and the best of those to Oxford in England for more learning. We have an active breeding program and our horses, sheep and cattle are in big demand, commanding the highest prices. We use the most modern methods to farm our crops. All of our people, male and female, are educated, even the poorest. We have many tradesmen and produce all of our own machinery. Like your father's people, all of our males serve a minimum of five years in the army. Many choose to stay full time and we are often called upon by the government to supply troops.

"We threaten no one," he continued, after taking another sip from his glass. "The amount of poppy we grow is small and does not threaten the other tribes. They value our food production and the machinery we produce. A few warlords have been foolish enough to try and challenge us, but after they suffer massive losses, they stop. Other than the odd raid now and then from across the border, we are generally left alone. And those raids are small and infrequent and generally unsuccessful. The border tribes have learned to their great sadness that our retribution for those raids is swift and very, very deadly. We also cut off all trade to those people, and they suffer from that as well.

"We do not raid or seek to expand our lands. The others respect this as well. It is as your great father said. We live in peace and are friends to all."

"I have been with these people for but a short time," the Indian said to the raj. "They, like we, owe allegiance to the British Crown, but they prosper, while we do not. They treat us like equals, not like the British do. They respect our talents and culture and do not push theirs on us. They teach us much and share their knowledge freely. They have many women among them, who are respected and treated as equals. One is even a mighty warrior. I have seen her in action: she is as fierce as any of the men – and General, she should be commanding a troop, not serving as a lowly gunner."

"I will take that under advisement, Colonel," John said. "But her commander and the RSM must agree first. Colonel Bashir," he went on. "I see that your weapons are British. We had thought to supply you with two hundred Mauser rifles and twenty Maxim machine guns."

"The British have been very competitive in their pricing," Bashir said. "But they balk at supplying us with automatic weapons. What would be the cost of these weapons?"

"Well," John said, a grin on his face. "Some Turks we ran into decided they no longer needed them, so they gave them to us. Where we are going we won't need them either and they are taking up a lot of valuable space. I think we can let you have them for the price of a feast and camping for two nights. We only have the ammunition the Turks gave us, though, so you will have to arrange for more."

"In that case we will take them all of course," Bashir said. "We too have found the Turks to be very generous when they run away. Ammunition will not be a problem. Our artisans are very skillful. We manufacture most of our own right now. The supplies you provide will give my people enough knowledge to make replacement ammunition and parts. The feast is being laid out and I see you already have a nice camp spot."

"One more thing," John said. "If possible, I would like to parade and honor our dead, sir. Perhaps before the feast?"

"But of course," Bashir said. "You have but to ask if you need anything from us. I see your people are coming back from the field, and some anxious-looking young men awaiting your attention. I too must return to my duties. Until tonight then?"

As Bashir walked away, four dusty scout cars and eight armored cars came into camp in a roar of engines and clouds of dust. The patrols had come back in. A signals captain approached and handed a message to John.

"The British are wondering when we will be in port, sir," the captain said.

"Let them know we are doing repairs and resting for the next two days," John said. "They won't know any different and probably expect it anyway. Also let them know all offensive operations have halted, but we will still fire if fired upon. Colonel," he said to the Indian. "You are welcome to join the parade if you wish. Your people have fought with us and were here at this battle. If you would be so kind as to spread the word to my people? Full parade, if you please. And Hood, clean up my command car as good as you can and have it ready behind the graves for when we arrive. One of these nice people Bashir has supplied us will show you where."

At four pm, John walked out of his tent, dark blue dress uniform buttoned up, highly polished brown cavalry boots laced up the front, wearing his Colt pistol and belt, pistol on the left, butt forward. Six highly polished pistol cartridges sat in red loops on the left side of his tunic, six rifle cartridges in loops on the right. The hilt of a scabbarded sword poked over his left shoulder, his full-sized medals were arranged on his chest and, today, a Stetson hat squared away on his head.

All of the troops had been lounging in front of their tents, waiting for his arrival, and as he emerged, they formed up in front of the tents. All of them were dressed as John was, in full dress-blue uniforms, cavalry boots, Stetson hats, medals and weapons. John nodded and the bugler sounded assembly. The troopers converged into their companies and battalions. The color party formed up in front of John and he nodded again and led them out of the camp to the small gravesite.

He halted them so that the center of the formation was across from the three graves; the Indians were on the left of the formation and a large contingent of townspeople were watching at a respectful distance. John marched up to his gleaming command car and climbed to the roof, taking the cone shaped hand voice magnifier from Major Hood.

"Troopers," he said, his voice clear on voice magnifier. "All of us have heard the stories of that great battle so many years ago. Now all of us have seen the battlefield. Have heard and seen how the battle progressed. Now you know how truly courageous our ancestors were. How outnumbered they were. How they did their best and prevailed. Like us today, they were far from home and with no support. Despite all of that and with the help of the local people we were able to prevail. Again, like today.

"These three people gave their lives so that we might be free. So that we can be who we want to be, not who we are told to be. So that our descendants can live a life of freedom and choice. We owe everything to these people and their sacrifice.

"Soon, some of us will be going to help more of our people. Helping those who are being persecuted, and bringing them home with us. Have no doubt in your minds. That country has no love for us. They will challenge us; they will test us. But we will prevail. For we are Canadian, we are Andreas Host. We are the best of the best, the toughest of the toughest and we owe it all to these three people.

"We have buried friends in Palestine, in Africa and here, in Afghanistan. The price of freedom is often paid in blood. Never forget the sacrifices of those who have paid that price."

Then he called them to attention and the Last Post rang out from four buglers and the regiment's color was lowered in salute. More than a few rifles and arms were quivering as they held the salutes while the bugles sounded, and tears were flowing freely down cheeks. John held them silent for a few seconds as the last notes echoed from the town walls.

"Comrades," he said, now in German. "Soon we will be in France. We will fight relatives and friends from the Fatherland. They will fight hard. They will be defending their homes. But if we do not stop them, they will take from us the freedoms we have fought so hard to gain. We cannot let them take those freedoms away, freedoms so many of us have paid for. Color party front and center!" He yelled now in Russian.

The four veterans slow marched across the formation, not the way the regiment did now, but in the Russian fashion. Left arms swinging across their chests, legs coming belt high. Bashir had lent them one of the old original colors, which the veteran medical captain bore with pride, her head held high and a Winchester across her back. The other two Bears flanked her, Winchesters on their shoulders and the RSM led from the center, Winchester across his back and a sword held upright in his right hand. They arranged themselves in front of the command vehicle and behind the graves, facing the regiment. Standing at rigid attention, they had black lamb's wool caps on instead of Stetsons, all cocked back on the crowns of their heads.

"Brothers and sisters," John said in English. "We have all seen the battlefield. We have all seen the piles of spent cartridges, the mass of bones where the enemy fell. Our motto came after Africa, but it was born here. Determination Against All Odds!"

John had thought he would have to prompt them again, but the whole regiment belted it right back at him. It was so loud, birds rose in flight and the ground trembled. Then he climbed down from the truck and marched to the head of the regimental color party. He led them to the far right of the formation and had the regiment face right. Then he led the regiment in a long left curve so that they were marching to the left of the graves and the color party of veterans; he started to sing, and the regiment followed suit, the regimental song. The verses matched the pace of the march, quick, almost a trot. No orders were necessary as each column of eight came abreast of the graves, all eight heads snapped right and swords presented to the honor party.

When the last Indian trooper had passed, the captain holding the flag collapsed to her knees, put her head on her arms and wailed. Ivanca had been with Irene as a captive so many years before – they had been lifelong friends and she had been with her when she died.

John had extracted himself from the officers' party as soon as he could without upsetting anyone. Nobody really noticed he had gone anyway. Everyone was singing and dancing and the vodka was flowing freely, so it was easy to disappear. He wandered through the different tents, accepting drinks, but drinking little. Soon he found himself at a set of horse corrals. He put a foot on a bottom rail and leaned his arms on the top rail looking at the animals milling about.

Soon his mind was drifting to another corral far away and surrounded by trees. The sound of his nieces and nephews playing in his ears and the smell of his mother's cooking in his nose. I have to break myself of that, he thought. No time to be homesick. I hope things are not as bad as we are being told it is in Russia. Or in France. I don't know how many more I can bury.

Then he shook his head, undid the buttons from his

tunic and a couple of buttons from his shirt. Shoving his Stetson to the back of head, he lit a cigar and sauntered back to his tent.

"Just like his father," Ivanca said, passing the vodka bottle over to the RSM. They had been sitting quietly, backs against a feed stall, unseen by John.

"Ya, a little," the RSM said. "But I think he is tougher. He has no fear that one. If I don't keep an eye on him he will get himself killed. Then where would we be? His brother has no head for this and Andreas is getting too old. We need this kid."

"We need to find him a woman," Ivanca said. "Someone as tough as he but more refined. Someone to take the rough edges off."

"It hasn't been for lack of effort, Ivanca," the RSM said. "He's had more than his fair share of ladies, I can tell you. Maybe if Yonny or Ivan or even Katia were here they could talk some sense into him."

"I will have a talk with Willy and Susan when we reach France," Ivanca said. "They will straighten him up."

Chapter Seven

The next day was a write off, most of the troops being in no condition to even get out of bed in the morning. But John had them on the road just after dawn the following day and they reached the sleepy port town in Iran ten days later, men and machines dusty, tired and in need of repair.

"General," said Colonel Makarov. "Are you sure you going to Odessa is necessary? It would be better if you were to go with the main body to France."

"I appreciate your concern, Colonel," replied John. "This has been discussed with our high command and it is felt my personal contacts as well as rank will be required in Odessa. As I said, Stephan will take temporary command until I reach France. He commanded the regiment in Africa, so has field experience under combat conditions, and has been in France for two years now, so knows how to deal with the Allied command structure. He also outranks me: he's a lieutenant general, so it will be hard to push him around. No, take the time to rest and train the troops in their new role. When I arrive and resume command, they will want us to get into action immediately, so I am relying on you to prepare the troops properly."

"Very well," said the colonel. "Are you sure you want to take the worst vehicles?"

"As long as they work, I want them," said John. "I am not expecting much in the way of trouble and I don't think they will be coming back with us. I know how the Russian mind works. I'd rather they got the worn out trucks than the good ones."

The vehicles, arms and supplies were loaded on their transports, troopers were filing into theirs and John and his small staff were ready to embark on the British Navy Cruiser for the one-day sail to Odessa. This would be the first time the regiment had been separated since landing in the Middle East and the first time John had ever been on a large armed vessel. The size of the armaments was impressive to a man who thought of field guns as heavy weapons. His batteries looked like toys compared to even the smallest of the big guns the cruiser carried.

The weather was warm and the seas calm, and the small convoy reached Odessa at first light. A boat pulled away with a landing party of British Naval Officers, while the big cruiser and the rest of the convoy anchored in the harbor. The initial excitement of landing had given way to boredom as the day dragged on with no response from the landing party. Awnings were broken out to shade the decks of the ships as the climbing sun began to burn skins and raise tempers.

On the third morning of riding at anchor in the harbor, the landing parties arriving each evening in frustration, John decided to take matters in his own hands, and received permission from the frustrated cruisers captain to send the RSM to shore with a message for the Russian in charge of the district. John followed the boat's progress and the short meeting the RSM had with the dock officials with his binoculars from the shore side of the cruiser's deck, smiling as the RSM slipped the official a bottle of vodka. The official gave the message to another man, who left in the direction of the town center, while he and the RSM walked over to a table and chairs set up in the shade of the customs building and shared the bottle. Less than an hour later the RSM was back on board and handed John a return message.

"All set for after lunch, General," Wilhelm reported.

"Right then," said John. "Dress uniform, pistol only if you please, RSM."

Both men reappeared on deck dressed in their blue dress uniforms, Colt 1911 pistols in holsters strapped to their left hips, butts forward.

"I wouldn't be very hopeful if I were you," said the captain of the cruiser. "This Mr Stalin is very stubborn and belligerent."

"I can only try," said John. "My troops on those transports will be suffering in this heat. If I can't get something arranged today or tomorrow, we might as well say it won't happen and head to France."

Disembarking from the motor launch at the dock, John and the RSM were greeted by a delegation of military and civilian representatives of the Bolshevik government, and, after the initial greetings, were escorted to a worn but serviceable motorcar and driven to the town hall. A delegation was waiting at the steps of the town hall and a man in military uniform greeted John warmly, speaking a Georgian-accented Russian.

"Welcome to Odessa, comrade General," the man said. "I am Stalin, the commissar for this district."

John waited as the greeting was translated into passable English by the man designated as interpreter by the Bolsheviks.

"It is a pleasure to meet you, comrade Stalin," said John in English. "I fear the Imperialist British may have given the wrong impression of the reason for my mission and I have come to express the wish of my government to assist you in ridding Mother Russia of the oppressing persons responsible for so much wrongdoing."

The RSM interpreted his words into Russian and Stalin raised an eyebrow and looked at his interpreter, who nodded that the translation was accurate.

"In that case, comrade General, perhaps we should go to my office and discuss how your government can assist us in this matter," said Stalin, pointedly ignoring the British Naval Commander who had accompanied the party.

John and the RSM were escorted into what had before been a plush boardroom, which now had all the lavish decorations removed, only the now badly scarred board table and chairs remaining. A red flag with a gold sickle and hammer in the corner was the only decoration in the room.

"Comrade Stalin," John began in Russian. "Now that the prying ears of the bourgeois British are not present, I can converse in the language that my mother taught me."

He nodded at the RSM, who reached into the brief case he was carrying and pulled out a fresh bottle of vodka and placed it on the table.

"This is from my homeland and I am sure it is not as good as what is produced in Mother Russia, but it is all I have, I am afraid," John said.

Stalin waved to an attendant, who produced several glasses, and the assembled men toasted each other's and their countries' health.

"We have heard and acknowledge the deeds and accomplishments of your father and mother, comrade Bekenbaum," Stalin said. "Indeed I attended the same seminary as your father and like him was disillusioned by the practices taught there. It is a pity your father had to leave Mother Russia."

"My parents did not like the direction the Boyars were taking and how they were treating our people, so he took advantage of an offer from our new country and we have prospered," replied John. "The protolerit of my people have elected me, though I am but a poor younger son, to represent and lead them when our country asked us to help remove the German Imperialist threat. I could not refuse the protolerit, even though I only wish to be back home tending my herds and crops."

The Bolsheviks at the table nodded at the wisdom and humility of the statement.

John produced a document from the briefcase and handed it to Stalin. "That is an authorization from your Central Committee, signed by Comrades Lenin and Trotsky, for me to remove how so many Boyars and old royalty you have here in Odessa and to have them transported to England. It also authorizes me to approach the, what do you call them, Kulaks?" John asked for qualification and received nods from Stalin and the rest. "To approach these Kulaks and give them an opportunity to resettle in my country, where it is hoped we can retrain them to become better members of the protolerate. In any case, they would be out of your hair and be our problem."

"I can see how that would be a benefit to us," Stalin said after a moment of thought. "But we have a concern of why you require one thousand armed troops to accomplish this? We could supply you with troops if you require them."

"As much of the territory we will be traveling is disputed and as the people we are meeting with distrust both parties, we feel that a neutral third party would be beneficial," said John. "Also, if the Kulaks become unruly on route to resettlement, we would be able to handle them easily."

"What of those who do not wish to resettle?" asked Stalin.

"I cannot force people to do what they do not wish to do," replied John. "If they wish to remain in Mother Russia, so be it. My father gave his people the same choice when he left."

"You have one hundred armored vehicles," said Stalin. "That is a formidable force."

"Again, comrade Stalin, they will be used only to

transport people and to defend ourselves if the Whites are foolish enough to resist us," replied John. "At the end of my mission, I intend to donate all the vehicles to your revolutionary cause."

"You would give us these vehicles?" asked Stalin. "No strings attached?"

"Only that you look favorably at Canada's government once you have completed in unifying Mother Russia under the Red Banner," John replied.

"If you and your senior sergeant would give us a few minutes, I will give you our answer, comrade Bekenbaum," Stalin said and they were escorted into the adjoining waiting room.

Less than ten minutes later, Stalin returned and gave them permission to begin unloading vehicles and troops and to begin the evacuation of the refugees. Collecting their British escort, the two Canadians headed back to the docks saying nothing and keeping their faces blank. Even when back on the British motor launch and headed back to the ship, John offered no explanation to the lower-ranked officers. Only once he had been ushered into the fleet captain's cabin did John tell the captain that they could begin unloading at the dock as soon as was possible.

"How did you manage that after one short meeting?"

the captain asked.

"I showed them the authorization papers from their central committee," John replied.

"But what if it had been the Whites instead of the Bolsheviks?" the captain asked. "You had no way of knowing who was in charge here when we left Iran."

"You're right: I had no way of knowing," replied John. "That's why I also had authorization papers from the Whites central committee. If I have your leave, sir, I must see that my troops are ready to disembark."

"You cagey bastard," the RSM said to John once they were alone on deck. "I was wondering why you were reading all that Communist manifesto and Marx and Lenin nonsense. I know you don't believe any of it. Comrade this and comrade that."

"Tell them what they want to hear, show them what they want to see," said John. "You really didn't believe those documents were real did you? So, I will accompany the first parties to both settlements. I know people in both places. After that we will see how it goes. Have the first group ashore set up camp and be ready to begin accepting refugees from the aristocrats. We just take down their names, billet them separately and hand them over to the Brits for processing. Knowing the Brits, it will take them sometime to get organized. The same thing with any refugees from the town: if we don't know them or they can't prove they are members of our Cossack groups, let the Brits handle them."

John told the officer in charge of unloading the vehicles that he wanted twenty of the real armored cars unloaded and ready to go first; he also wanted their crews and all the weapons. Both the national and regimental mobile colors were to be mounted on the lead car. He wanted the camp colors to be raised as soon as camp had been set up. Everyone was to wear dress uniform all the time. This was to distinguish them from the Brits and any of the opposing factions' troops. Everyone was to wear loaded sidearms and he ordered guard posts manned by Lewis gunners as well as riflemen with bayonets fixed. This was to be regarded as a hostile camp.

Christine asked permission to go and change into her dress uniform, which left Major Hood alone with John.

"Well, Major," John said. "It would appear that you are between a rock and a hard place. Unless you are wearing the regiment's dress uniform, I am afraid you will have to stay in camp."

"Unfortunately, General," said Alex. "Even if I had a regimental dress uniform, I would not be entitled to wear it."

"According to British regulations, you are entitled to

wear the uniform of any unit you are attached to for duty," John said. "The reports I received from your armored car crew inform me that you are competent in commanding that vehicle and that you have mastered all of the weapons. That entitles you to wear the uniform as far as regimental regulations are concerned."

John then waved his batman to come forward with the two sets of blue dress uniforms he was carrying. "Those are yours," he said. "Please look after them. They are hard to come by. Patching bullet holes and washing blood out of them are a pain."

John walked away and missed the startled look on the major's face as he saw the eagle shining on each uniform collar.

"Why, Father, don't you look nice in that brand new blue uniform?" John said to his uncle, who was wearing the regiment's blue uniform with a gold cross on the right collar.

"Much nicer than that faded old black thing he was wearing before," agreed Christine.

"Nice to see that both of you have the Bekenbaums' disrespectful trait," said Father Paul. "Now if I could only find some officers in this regiment who actually knew what they were doing."

"Ya ya," said John. "OK, so here is the plan. We are

going to Katherental first. I didn't spend too much time there on my trip here, but there should be a number of people there who remember you, Father. I will say my spiel, then go to Mother's hometown. I will leave ten troopers and a car with you and you can answer any questions the people have to ask. We should be back before three and will pick you up then."

"Sure, leave me behind in enemy country," Father Paul said with a grin.

"Christine, I do not know what we will come across. The areas between towns were dangerous when I was here in '05 and I have every reason to believe it is the true wild west out there now. Both sides may decide to take us on, so be ready. We won't start it, but I damn well mean to finish it."

By noon they pulled into Katherinetal in a cloud of dust and flags flying. The people were wary but many recognized Father Paul and few John. The town was a little more run down from what John remembered and the people more servile, but after several years of war and uncertainty this was to be expected. John spent an hour talking with the town's leaders, then left to head to old Vasilis's settlement.

When they stopped and stepped out of the cars, John noticed the gathered people were wary, almost afraid. The town was run down and several buildings had been burnt down. It wasn't until one of the old women recognized the regiment's flag and uniform, then John himself, and came running to embrace him, that the townspeople relaxed somewhat.

The town leaders told John that the war had been difficult on the settlement. Many of the men had died in the trenches, or had come home to starvation. The settlement had taken no part in any of the revolution or the civil war and, while the Whites had gone easy on them, the Bolsheviks had treated them harshly. Old Vasili and his nephew had been shot in front of the townspeople and they had taken what little food and livestock the people had. In the leaders' opinion, everyone in the settlement would take John's offer to resettle in Canada.

"Starting tomorrow," John said. "We will make two trips per day. We can take five hundred people and their luggage per trip. No furniture, no animals, only one package of belongings each, no bigger than one person can carry. We will provide you with lodging and food during the trip and once you reach our settlement in Canada you will be provided with animals, housing and furniture. The major here will be in charge of the evacuation; she has my authority and she speaks for me. Major," he turned to say to Christine, "have the troops pass out all the rations we have. These people need them more than we do."

The vehicles always had two days' rations for the troops on board and Christine soon had them unloaded and passed to the town leaders for distribution.

They returned to Katherintal just before three, and the priest and his crew were ready to go. To make room for Father Paul, Christine jumped out and got into the priest's vehicle and they were on their way.

"Stubborn fools those," said Father Paul. "The ones that are better off are staying. They believe all that nonsense the Bolsheviks are talking. The poorer ones are coming, about a thousand, maybe twelve hundred tops."

"They shot Vasili and his nephew in front of the towns people," John said quietly. "Then took most of their food and animals. We can count on three thousand from there. That's all that are left, three thousand. There were more than ten thousand when I was here in '05."

They spent the rest of the trip back to camp in Odessa in silence.

The next morning, earlier than expected, John was woken by angry loud voices demanding to see him. Taking his time, he dressed and casually exited the tent, grabbing the proffered cup of coffee and accepting a match to light his morning cigar. The people clamoring to see him had clearly at one time been well to do, for their clothing, while worn, was of good quality. John watched for a while, the people so engrossed in what they were doing that they had not noticed he was watching them. Finally, when they started shoving one another, trying to be first, he jumped onto his table, and pulling his Colt from its holster, fired two rounds into the air.

    Putting the pistol back in its holster, he pulled out the Canadian flag so everyone could see it and pointed to it. "Do you see this flag?" he yelled. "This is not the flag of Russia, or the Whites or the Bolsheviks. This is the flag of Canada. We only recognize King George the Fifth as our king. I take no orders other than those issued by him."

    He let that sink in for a minute, then continued. "Many of you mocked my father and my people. Some of you tried to have him and my people killed. Now you want me to save you? You have the right to apply for asylum, just as any other person in Russia does. You will follow our procedures and you will start by going to those tents over there and registering. We need your name and your status before the revolution. If we feel you may qualify, you will be given a chit to enter the camp for further processing."

Troopers with bayonets fixed on rifles appeared and began to shepherd the fallen aristocrats over to the processing area.

"Our minders seem to approve," said the RSM pointing at the Bolsheviks posted at the camp's entrance to keep an eye on them. They were pointing and raising vodka bottles in John's direction, many of them clapping.

"God willing, we are out of here in a week," John said.

"None to soon for me," the RSM agreed.

John was busy all morning doing the never ending battle with paperwork, his stomach growling and back hurting. He stood arching his back to ease the aches. Looking out at the line of refugees that now stretched to a quarter of a mile, he spotted a group of nine people that looked familiar. Like the rest, they were dressed in good clothing that had seen better days. At their head was a tall slender grandmother who still held herself erect. Two children of about four years of age held onto their fathers' pants legs, while two women had prams they were pushing. Each of the adults had one medium-sized travel bag on the ground beside them.

"Karl." John called over his aide for the day. "Do you

see that group over there with the two kids and prams? Have the RSM collect a squad and escort them to me if you will. Ralf," he said to his batman. "Tell the cook we will have five adults and two toddlers for lunch and see what he can do about baby formula or such for two infants. I am also going to need some decent quarters for two families."

Used to his commander's quirky nature, the long-suffering batman rushed to carry out the orders.

John watched as the bayonet-tipped riflemen made their way through the crowd to the small group. Instantly a vacant space was created around them as people moved to get out of the way or, more likely, not to be seen as associating with the group. A slight discussion was held between the older woman and the corporal in charge of the squad and, surrounded by the squad, the little group made its way to the headquarters area, heads down and steps hesitant.

John was in the process of clearing away his paperwork and had his back turned when the group reached his quarters; before the corporal of the squad could report, the elderly lady began to speak in clear Russian-accented and controlled English.

"My family and I have done nothing wrong sir," she said. "We were lined up quietly as we were told and were causing no trouble. There is no reason to single us out like this."

Turning around, John saw that she was doing her utmost to control her anger, but indignation was written all over her and her son was vainly grabbing her arm, trying to get her to be quiet.

"There was every reason to single you out, my lady," John said. "Bekenbaums never forget their friends, or people who have helped them out. Please have a seat, my lady. I am sure you could use some lunch, no?"

The grand lady – the marquise – now looked confused, and her son took the initiative, stepping forward and offering his hand.

"It's John, is it not?" the man said. "You remember, Mother, when the Bekenbaums were here in '05. He was the quiet one who only wanted to see the library and who was chaperone for his sisters."

"Why, so it is," the lady said, extending her hand to John. "Would you be able to put a good word in for us with the commander? I am afraid we have little or no influence here any longer."

John had them sit down and over lunch heard their tale of what had occurred during the months after the revolution. First, the Whites had kicked them out of their mansion and relieved her husband of his duties. They had lived in a small farmhouse on one of the nearby farms that they owned. Then the Bolsheviks had come, evicting them from the farm and confiscating everything but the clothes they were wearing. The Bolsheviks had forced the whole family to live in one small room in a hotel, where water and heat were nonexistent and food was scarce. One morning they had come with armed men, taken her husband out into the street, declared him an enemy of the state and had shot him in the middle of the street, as they had done with Vasili and many other leaders from the old days.

"My parents will be devastated when they hear the news of your husband's death, as am I, my lady," John said. "As far as using my influence, well, it all depends on you. If you wish to immigrate to Europe, I will vouch for you to the British commander. I can however, assure you that should you choose to come to Canada, there will be absolutely no problem."

"My son and son-in-law have some skill at managing farm workers and farming, but we have no money and no contacts outside Russia," the grand lady said. "I would not feel comfortable in Europe, being penniless. Do you think your father could help us in Canada?"

"If you are willing to come and work hard, learn new skills, I am sure that will be arranged," John said. "My parents have often remarked on your kindness and helpfulness to them. It is the least I can do to try and pay back all that my family owes yours. During the coming week, I will meet with your sons and they can fill me in on what they have to offer. Meanwhile I have arranged for accommodations for all of you. It is not much, but it is dry and warm; you will take your meals here with me, agreed?"

    The grateful former aristocrats were still expressing their appreciation to John as they were led away to their temporary quarters. He had just resumed his seat and taken a sip of coffee, when the first convoy of trucks bearing Katherental refugees arrived to the jeers and cat-calls of the observing gang of Bolsheviks. Unlike the aristocrats, these people were unloaded at the gates of the compound and escorted directly to the camp set up for them. Many had friends and relatives among the members of the regiment and their apprehension over the move soon dissolved into happy reunions, and the aid of new friends with cheerful faces helping them stow their meager possessions. As soon as they were unloaded, the trucks turned around and headed back for the next load.

    "There will only be one more trip," said Father Paul, accepting the offered cup of coffee from John. "Only a thousand agreed to come."

"It's their choice," John said. "I refuse to force them."

Before they had finished their coffee, the first convoy of the group from Vasyli's settlement arrived. This group was visibly relieved when they entered the camp and saw all the blue-uniformed armed troopers. For many, it must have been the first time in many months when they did not have to worry about being arrested and being killed. The trucks from this convoy also turned around as soon as the last refugee was unloaded and much more quickly sped out of town.

"Two more trips then," John said. "We should be finished by supper tomorrow."

The evening's meal was shared with the marquise and her family; she was already acquainted with Father Paul and John presented Alex and Christine to her. She was most interested in hearing of Christine's exploits as a military commander. Having a woman serve in the military was rare enough, but a woman commanding combat troops was unheard of.

"The commodore has assured me that the conversion of the ships that carried the vehicles to refugee transport is almost complete," Alex said. "Arrangements have been made for two destroyers to escort them and us to Gibraltar, then we will proceed in convoy to France and a couple of Canadian escorts will get the refugees through Panama and to

Vancouver."

"Any time frame?" asked John.

"We can sail in three days," Alex replied.

"Very well," John said. "Have the RSM start loading the groups that came in today in the morning and as many of our supplies as he can."

The next day, John was too busy to socialize. He was supervising the loading of equipment and refugees into the transports and fielding myriad inquiries from the British on how they should proceed with processing their refugees. That poor lot were huddled under whatever protection from the elements they could find or manufacture. Finally he told the British that they could have the Canadian tents and rations after they had left. He ordered his quartermaster to give the British the one hundred tents they had not needed and which were still in their packing crates, but the Brits could come and get them themselves.

Just before dinner, John was able to observe the last refugee column arrive. The first fifty trucks had already unloaded their charges and were parked in neat rows in the assembly area reserved for them. Troopers were busy removing radios, ammunition and arms from them and carrying them to the quartermaster's area, where they were cataloged and crated.

As the last truck unloaded the last passenger, before the RSM muttered, "Oh shit, there's trouble," John was on the move, quickly headed for the gate, unbuckling the flap of his pistol holster as he went.

The last passenger was a good-looking tall woman in her early twenties. She was dressed in clothing that clearly set her apart from her fellow refugees and unlike them carried no luggage, though there was a suspicious thickening around her waist and hips. She walked quickly with the others, keeping her head down, but it was clear that she did not belong. From the shine of her hair to the very good leather of her boots, this woman was not a Cossack. This fact was also evident to the commissar of the Bolshevik group assembled outside the camp gate, and he swung into motion, grabbing the woman by the arm and pulling her roughly out of the line of refugees, who were now scattering at a run for the gate.

As John passed the gate, he gave the prepare-for-action signal with his right arm over his head to any troopers who could see him and strode directly to the commissar and his captive.

"What is going on here?" John demanded of the commissar.

"This woman is clearly an unregistered boyar and one

of high status, unlike those dirty Kulaks you have been collecting," the man replied haughtily. "If you try to interfere I will have you shot!"

John pulled his Colt automatic from his holster and putting it over his head so that his men could see him chambering a round into it, he leveled the pistol at the commissar's head. "If you think losing your life over a tall, overdressed and overweight woman is worth it, who am I to disagree? By the time your four men level their rifles, you and two of them will be dead and my Lewis gunners will then shred the other two to pieces. This woman was on one of my trucks, which means she is under my protection. Now let her go before I get angry and shoot you just for standing there."

As the dismayed commissar heard the cocking of Lewis guns and rifles all around him, he let go of the woman's arm and she scurried behind John's back.

"Comrade Stalin shall hear of this," the man said defiantly.

"Good," John said with a wicked smile. "You can also tell Comrade Stalin that I am not pleased and that you have jeopardized my decision to hand over all these vehicles to him. Ask him if he thinks one overweight and overdressed woman is worth losing one hundred trucks."

Putting the pistol on safe and holstering it, he took the now shaking woman's arm in his and walked to his headquarters with her. With each step she took further away from the gate, she regained composure until, by the time they reached John's quarters, she was walking erect, head high. John pulled out a chair for her at the table, bidding her to sit down.

"Let me guess," Ralf said with a sigh. "One more for dinner."

John sat at the opposite end of the table from her, both of them sizing up the other. She had blond hair and blue eyes, her shoulders and hips were slender, which did not explain the thickness of her of her middle, which seemed to go right around.

"Is it true, the saying of your people?" she asked. Her voice was exquisite to hear and her Russian was definitely upper class. "Once you have saved someone, you are responsible for them?"

"I have already said that I am responsible for you," John replied. "Do you have any people I can contact who may be worried about you? Your mother and father, or siblings perhaps?"

"No there is no one, they are all gone," she replied. "What little I had, I used to bribe the guards to let me on that truck."

"You bribed my people!" John growled. "I will have their asses for that!" the last was in English and as he rose to summon his aide, she quickly put her hand on his arm. A feeling like a shot of electricity shot up John's arm, the hair rising on it, as she gently removed her hand.

"Please, your people did no wrong, sir," she said in entrancing Russian-accented English. "I bribed the Bolsheviks guarding the camp."

"Oh, that's different then," John said. "I hope you did not have to pay too big a price."

"Oh no sir, my virginity is still intact," she said matter-of-factly. "I gave them my last ring, is all."

"Well then, my lady, I am John Bekenbaum and I have the pleasure of commanding this tiny detachment," John said. "And you are?"

"My name is Tatiana Romanovchuk; my parents were of the old royalty," she said. "Your father is Andreas and your mother Elizabeth? Heroes of Russia both? I am so lucky to have a rich and powerful man as my protector."

"You are correct in who my parents are," John agreed. "But I am the youngest of four: my older brother inherits everything and I am but a poor farmer. In my country, a man must make it on his own, not like here.

Names and titles mean nothing there, or among us here. We are judged on our actions and deeds, not on who we are related to."

Before she could reply, they were joined by the marquise and her family. The marquise looked at the young woman and was about to say something when a gesture unseen by John by the young lady stopped her from speaking.

John made the introductions to the group and Christine sat next to Tatiana. The two were soon in deep conversation and John was free to enjoy his meal and conversation with the whole group. As the evening went on he felt Tatiana's eyes on him more than once and he caught himself looking at her more than once.

Watch yourself, laddy, he thought. You know nothing of this woman, and now is not the time or place anyway.

"John?" Christine said, gaining his attention. "Tatiana tells me she is a trained nurse and served in a hospital in St Petersburg looking after the wounded. We could use her: we are really short staffed."

"Oh yes, sir," Tatiana said. "I would be ever so happy to be given an opportunity to be useful."

"Well that solves a couple of problems for me," John said. "All right, Major, she can bunk in with you when she is not on duty. Have her enlisted as a sub lieutenant for now, temporary non-combat approved. See if you can find her a uniform, no badges. You will have to swear an oath of loyalty to the regiment," he told Tatiana. "Will you have a problem with that?"

"No, sir," she replied.

"I will have her qualified for her Bear in no time," Christine said.

"Do you know what that means, getting your Bear?" John asked Tatiana.

"Yes sir, the major has just explained it to me," she replied.

"There is more to it than simply qualifying at weapons," John said. "It means leaving everything else behind and devoting yourself to the regiment and to Canada. Don't rush into it. Take the training, spend some time with us before you make your decision."

"Thank you, sir," Tatiana said.

The sun had gone down and everyone was tired, so the groups broke off and headed for their quarters. John thought it odd that the marquise, normally an active member during the dinner discussions, was silent tonight. Even stranger, she accompanied the two younger women as they left, walking behind and not beside them. Must be a woman thing, he thought, shrugging his shoulders and taking a last puff of his cigar. He went to bed.

It was not until they had anchored at Gibraltar that John had an opportunity to observe his new charge, sub lieutenant Romanovchuk. He had been kept busy processing reports and reading of the situation in France, so busy that he rarely had an opportunity to get on the deck of the British destroyer he and his headquarters party were billeted on. Now that they were at anchor, he had finally taken the time to get some fresh air and walk about the deck. He joined his twenty-five troopers in their Tai Chi exercises for the first time since Afghanistan and was sweating heavily at the end of the one-hour work out. Heading to the bow, he noticed the two women sparring with wooden swords: they were both skilled and evenly matched.

 The clothing Tatiana had been wearing when she arrived in the refugee camp had been replaced by the khaki uniform they all wore now they were no longer in Russia. John noticed that she was a great deal slimmer than she had been. Her long legs, no longer hidden under skirts, only accented the trim waist line she had. Her long blond hair, like Christine's, was braided and bound up in a pony-tail that hung down to the middle of her back to end just above her belt line. Her technique with the sword was more classical than Christine's, which indicated she had been tutored in the art by a true sword master. But she could not get the better of the more clumsy-looking Christine, who had been trained in the art as a soldier, not a duelist.

They finished their routine and hugged each other, beaming and glowing from the exercise, and Christine noticed him watching them, said something to Tatiana and came up to John.

"She really is quite good with the sword, cousin," Christine said. "She is teaching me and could put me down any time she wants. Why don't you give her a try? She could use some better competition."

John agreed and took Christine's practice weapon from her, making a few cuts to get the feeling of the blade. He had not worked with swords since leaving Didsbury and it might be fun and even humiliating for him to take on a classically trained opponent. Grasping the sword hilt in both hands, he presented it before his face and bowed to Tatiana, who nodded back in return, giving the slashing swipe that duelists used as a salute. She turned sideways, pointing her right-handed sword point, her left arm arched behind and above her head and her knees bent. John also turned sideways, both hands still on the sword hilt, sword held before him, knees bent, feet shoulder width apart in a mimic of the Tai Chi exercises he had just completed.

She came at him unexpectedly and fast, lunging her point at his chest; John swept her sword away, dancing to one side and clipping her gently on her rear with his sword as he walked away out of reach. More wary this time she feinted to his mid-section before going for his eyes; once again John swept her sword aside with his, spinning away and tapping her this time on the back of the knee with his sword as he went by. Now she was clearly confused and went on the defensive, forcing John to go to her.

John, in a slow-looking move, pulled the sword to the left side of his head, point up, and gracefully swept it toward her left side, then, as she moved to block it, changed to a lunge and caught her between her breasts, before once again sweeping her sword aside and dancing away untouched. He could see she was becoming agitated and upset at what he was doing, and she suddenly and in a blur of motion attacked again, this time cutting at his head. John turned to the side and took one hand off the sword, swatting hers out of danger with his, caught her sword arm with his free hand under her elbow, and gently twisted her to fall over the leg he had extended behind her knee, forcing her to the deck on her back. He held her right arm, still holding the sword with his left hand, extended up and out of harm's way, while his right brought his sword to her come to a rest on her neck, point just beneath her chin. She could do nothing and knew it, dropping her sword and conceding the match.

John helped her to her feet and once again placing both hands on his sword hilt, point up and before his face, and bowed from the waist.

"Not bad for a rookie," he said tossing his sword at her. "She needs more work, Major," and he walked away, back to his cabin, her scent and the heave of her breasts while she was lying on the deck haunting him.

"He definitely likes you," Christine said, comforting an out-of-breath Tatiana.

"He humiliated me!" Tatiana said indignantly.

"Oh no he didn't," Christine said, laughing. "When he spars with me I have bruises on my rump and my ribs and he tosses me on the ground, not the nice gentle push he gave you. You made him work harder than most of us, though."

"What is that style he is using?" Tatiana asked. "I have never seen that before."

"It is an Oriental technique we have adapted for our own use," Christine answered. "It melds the Tai Chi moves we train with a Japanese style of sword work. The only people I have seen who are as good as him at it are his brother Stephan, my father, his parents and my stepsister Susan."

"Women and old people as good as he?" Tatiana asked.

"It's not about strength or speed," Christine said. "It is about clarity of the mind and connecting the mind with the body, while using your opponent's strength against them. You have been trained well and you make me look foolish with your style, but you must remember, we are trained for combat and to kill via the most economical and efficient means possible. Using your methods on a battlefield would see you dead quickly."

"Then I must learn your methods," Tatiana said. "Now, don't you agree that John has the most adorable blue eyes you have ever seen, Chris?"

"Never noticed him that way: he is my first cousin after all."

"Oh and the way he walks, such grace."

"You're not looking at how he walks," Christine said. "You're just looking at his cute derriere"

"Why that too, of course." Tatiana laughed. "Is it true that he is just a farmer? His father is leaving nothing for him?"

"That was his choice, Tat," answered Christine. "He wants to make his own mark on the world and not use his father's and brother's reputation. His parents and siblings admire him for it and are quite proud of him, though they will never tell anyone outside the family that. He does very well for himself and has a number of interests that are doing well outside of the farming."

"Major, you have told me much of what I must do to become a member of your community," Tatiana said, and Christine knew that the use of her rank meant the conversation had turned serious. "I have thought hard and, if you think I am worthy, would you consider being my sponsor?"

"You are willing to renounce all your past life and allegiances?" asked Christine. "To swear allegiance to King George, Canada and the regiment? To serve your term of duty, without question?"

"Yes, Major Bekenbaum," Tatiana answered, now standing at attention.

"Very well probationary Sub-Lieutenant Romanovchuk, I would be happy to sponsor you for membership in our band, and will present your written submission to the general for his consideration."

At ten the next morning, John received a knock on the door to his small cabin and was surprised to see not only Christine but the RSM enter, dressed in their dress uniforms.

"General," Christine said, formally at attention. "I have a request for admission to the band for your consideration, sir!"

"General Bekenbaum, sir!" barked the RSM. "I have a request for admission to the band for your consideration, sir!"

John rose and held out his hand for the sealed written requests and watched as they about-faced and left, closing the cabin door gently behind them.

Opening the RSM's candidate's request first, he was surprised to see that Major Hood was asking for full admission to the band. His cousin-in-law Lionel had not even done that. He was a band member by marriage to John's cousin Susan. Christine's was no surprise. Tatiana's hand was fluid and graceful, betraying her good education. *There is more to this woman than she is letting on*, he thought.

He had the two candidates and their sponsors brought before him and the twenty other band members on deck that afternoon. All of them were wearing their blue dress uniforms.

"Candidate Hood, you are aware that you will have to

relinquish your rank and position in the Coldstream Guards regiment?" John asked.

"Sir, yes sir!" Alex bellowed out, standing rigidly at attention like a recruit at basic training.

"RSM?" John asked.

"General, sir!" the RSM said. "Candidate Hood has qualified expert on all our weapons. As a member of an elite British cavalry formation, his horsemanship will be excellent. He has proven reliable in combat and has shown superior leadership skills, sir!"

"Candidate Romanovchuk, you are aware of the duties and responsibilities that come with membership in our band and are willing to accept them and renounce all forms of former allegiance?"

"Sir, yes sir!" Tatiana, also at rigid attention, belted out.

"Major Bekenbaum?"

"Sir!" Christine began. "Candidate Romanovchuk has demonstrated skill in firearms and is an outstanding swordsman. She professes to be an expert rider and has trained with the Life Guards Cavalry regiment. Her commander at the hospital reports she is well trained and more than competent at her job, and is excellent at organizing and in leadership capabilities. The candidate is willing to undergo the traditional test of arms to prove she is a worthy candidate for band membership, sir!"

"Brothers, what say you?" John said in German, turning to the twenty band members at his back.

They converged, having a quiet conversation for a few moments, while the candidates and their sponsors stayed standing in line at attention. The group reformed, the two lines also at attention, and the least senior corporal took two steps forward saluted and said, "We have no problem with the candidates, General, sir!" then saluted and rejoined the line.

"Very well," said John to the group, then smartly about-faced and addressed the small line before him. "Candidate Hood, you and your sponsor shall present yourselves to a meeting of all band members at your earliest convenience upon our reunion with our brothers and sisters in France. Candidate Romanovchuk, at your earliest convenience upon our arrival in France, you and your sponsor shall present yourselves and you will demonstrate your skill in the traditional manner in front of the assembled members of the band, and will stand to hear their verdict. Dismissed," John finished, and pulled his cap to the back of his head as he preferred, and walked to the railing, looking out at the harbor.

"Thank you, John," Christine said, standing beside him. "I will have her ready in time."

"Is she good enough?" John asked. "She is qualified just with her skills as a nurse. The doctor says she is better than all his girls and has even shown him some techniques he was unaware of. He feels she could pass the doctors' exam easily."

"She wants her eagle, John," Christine said. "Who am I of anyone to deny her?"

"What do you think, RSM?" John asked as Wilhelm came to stand at his other side.

"If she trained with the Life Guards as she says, she should be OK," the RSM replied. "She shoots well even from the deck of this ship. I will have a chat with the other sergeants when we reach the regiment. I think she should be a member of the band, and she already qualifies as a Bear."

"All right; thank you for your comments, both of you," John said. "Christine, you and she are to report to me on deck each morning for two hours of training. And please tell her that it is going to be intense, not like this morning's playing."

The next morning John was on deck before they were, barefoot and dressed in an old set of loose combat fatigues. He greeted both women, then started explaining why it was so important to perform the Tai Chi movements. That the exercises brought mind and body into focus and that muscle memory would serve in times of stress and danger. He put them through an hour of exercise before explaining the intricacies of the sword skills he utilized and the reasoning behind them. Then he had the two women perform slow motion sequences not unlike the Tai Chi movements with the practice swords.

After a half hour he stopped them and had them join him sitting cross-legged on the deck. John then explained how these exercises would help Tatiana in her test. To make time slow down and become one with horse and firearm. To feel the exact moment when all four of the horse's hooves were off the ground, then firing at the target, much like shooting from the pitching deck of the destroyer. He recommended she visualize, in the first moments when she went to bed every night, the actions she would have to take while on horseback to complete her task. Then he rose, bowed to both of them, hands clenched to his chest, and left to prepare for the day's agenda.

Chapter Eight

John spotted his brother on the dock as he was walking down the gangway, and gave him a sloppy salute before the men embraced each other in a long hug.

"Damn, look at you, all tanned and fit," Stephan said.

"Well some of us have to work for a living while others sit around on their ample asses doing make-work projects," John replied laughing.

"Ah, cousin Christine, still as lovely as ever," Stephan said hugging her just as fiercely as he had hugged John earlier.

"Just as deadly too," she said kissing him on the cheek. "How are Mother and Susan?"

"Both fully recovered and working as hard as ever," Stephan answered. "They will be joining us for dinner. You have made quite the reputation as a no-nonsense Bosh killer John; Currie can't wait to get the troops on the line."

"Ah, dinner first, eh?" John said. "I will be back at work soon enough. Listen, Stephan, we have two candidates for band membership: one male, one female. Both of them are shoe-ins. The Englishman has proven combat skills and the Russian girl is superior in the medical department."

"If you are recommending them it should not be a problem," Stephan said.

"Well, there is one small fly in the ointment," John said. "The woman has requested a testing in the old way. She wants her eagle, and wants to prove to us she is worthy."

"Is she good enough?" Stephan asked Christine.

"John and I have been coaching her, she will be all right as long as she can ride as well as she says she can," Christine said. "Are there any good cavalry mounts around for us to borrow?"

"The Strathconas are quartered next to us," Stephan said. "I will ask them to lend us some mounts. Will two days be enough, do you think? We hold the test the evening of the second day, then the ceremonies after?"

"Should be long enough," John said. "I am bringing her to dinner; she is Christine's aide as of now. Perhaps Aunt Willy and Susan could give her some tips."

The four women bonded almost immediately and left the dinner table early, leaving John and Stephan to catch up on the three years they had been separated.

The two days passed quickly and, as John had predicted, Tatiana passed her test without dismounting. The shots were not as deadly as the other three women had done passing their tests, but still better than most who attempted it.

After the formal acceptance ceremony, a party broke out, but after a while John broke away from the celebrations, intent on spending some time alone. As he approached the edge of their camp, he heard quiet sobbing coming from a figure sitting on the ground, grabbing its knees and rocking back and forth. By the long hair and the flash of moonlight on the brass on her collar, John knew it was Tatiana. He quietly sat beside her, not intruding on her space until she looked up and over at him, then buried her face in his chest. John put one arm around her and stroked her hair with his other hand until she stopped crying and looked up at him, blue eyes sparkling in the moonlight.

"I am sorry, General," she said. "I was thinking of my sisters and little brother, and how proud they would be of me today – and how much I miss them."

"It's OK, Tat," John said using Christine's nickname for her for the first time. "You have a new family now, one that will love you as much as your old one did."

The next morning, hungover and sleep deprived, they were marched to a waiting troop train and were on their way to the killing fields of Europe.

"Welcome to the Western Front, gentlemen," said General Arthur Currie, the overall commander of the

Canadian Corps and the Allied troops in that sector. "We have a job that is well suited to your abilities and experience."

Arthur Currie had risen from an obscure militia gunner to one of the most brilliant military minds the Allies had. To the chagrin of the British and French officer class, he was not a professional soldier, or from the landed gentry class. He was a self-made businessman and part-time soldier.

Currie outlined the current situation on the front. The Germans had retreated behind the Rhine River, political upheaval had seen the Kaiser abdicate, and the civilian government was actively pursuing ceasefire talks. It was felt that by the middle of the month, the war would be over, but the German army was still fighting hard and particularly in the Cologne area.

Currie wanted the regiment to cross the Rhine and secure the bridge leading into Cologne. The Canadian Corps would be using Cologne as its base after the ceasefire had been signed. John's expertise in the area was crucial at this point. Although they had good maps and aerial photographs, nothing beat having actually been over the ground, as John had been during his visit thirteen years earlier. The Australians operating in that sector had run into fierce opposition, indeed bordering on the fanatical. It was crucial that John cross the Rhine and put pressure on the Germans from Germany itself. He was to contact the Australian commander for the latest information on the sector and to begin operations as soon as he was able.

A staff car was waiting and took John and Colonel Makarov to the Australian headquarters, where they met the same general they had worked with in Syria. He showed them his lines and the aerial photos of the German positions on the east side of the Rhine bridge. The Germans had dug themselves in and all approaches to the bridge were well defended from attack across it. John asked about a smaller bridge five miles to the north, and the Australian told him that was in the French and American sector, but they were held up three miles to the west. The situation was fluid and it was hard to tell what the French would be doing. He could give John aerials of the area by that afternoon. In the meantime, the three officers traveled to an observation point so the Canadians could take a look at what the Germans had to offer. The German positions were well located and manned. It would take a costly assault across the bridge to just establish a bridgehead. Then the city itself was well defended. Returning to the Australian headquarters, John thanked the general for the information, the two Canadians gathered up all the maps and photos and were driven back to their own headquarters.

John gathered his staff and spread the maps and the photos on tables, floors, walls – anything that could give them an area to look. Taking a magnifying glass to photos of Cologne, he looked mostly to the rear of the city and the approaches to it from the bridge five miles to the north. Then he examined the bridge area itself. Both sides of the span were fortified, but lightly manned, the nearest reserve troops being the ones facing the French and Americans three miles to the west and from Cologne itself. The Germans felt confident the little bridge was secure so John felt he had them where he wanted them; he began to outline his plan.

John stood looking out at the seated general officers and their staffs from all the surrounding Allied-controlled areas. Then looking to make sure the map was visible to all of them, he took up the pointer and began his briefing. "Gentlemen, the night of November 8, my regiment will move up to staging areas here, on the north flank of the Australian line. At midnight, five companies of dismounted troops will cross the line here and make their way five miles north to this bridge. We will secure the west side of the bridge, then cross and establish a bridgehead on the east side. Once that is accomplished, the rest of the regiment, mounted, will proceed to the bridge, cross it, and begin operations behind enemy lines. By midmorning, we expect to be in position to assault the rear of the German line protecting the Cologne Bridge."

"At daybreak, we would like demonstrations and artillery barrages all along the German lines in this sector, making the Germans think a major assault is in the works. Once the regiment attacks the rear, the Australians can, if they wish, begin an assault on the bridge and the city. If Allied forces could hold the small bridge, and the assault on Cologne and its bridge is successful, we will have cut off all the enemy troops in this area and established two footholds in Germany itself, ready for further exploitation."

"Right," said Currie after John had finished. "Make it happen, gentlemen. God willing it will be the last of the war."

The Australian general approached John outside and handed him a photograph.

"I want you to see who and what you will be fighting," he said. "We discovered them lying in a ditch after repulsing a counter-attack. The Germans were crossing the bridge after and laughing about it. It's the same bloody bastards we faced in Syria. The bloody Brits let them go."

The picture showed ten Australian soldiers lying in the ditch, hands tied behind their backs, each man shot behind the left ear.

"Death's Head insignia on caps and uniforms?" John asked. "Can you get me eight blown-up copies of this photo?"

The sun was going down as the convoys reached the staging area and the troopers dismounted the trucks and gathered in their groups, while their officers stood together, waiting for word to go. The eight majors and four colonels of the regiment converged on John's command vehicle for the last briefing.

"You all know what your jobs are and how to do them, nothing has changed in that regard," John said. "Once we cross this line, all communication, unless in code, is in German. That includes troopers talking to each other. Once the regiment crosses the bridge, in the dark, the enemy should take us for reinforcements and, until we hit them, I want them to keep thinking that way. Colonel, please hand one copy of these photos to each major. I want every trooper to see these pictures and what treatment they can expect from the enemy. During the initial phase of the attack, we have no time for prisoners. If all I see at the end of the attack are dead Death's Heads, so be it. Currie told me that even our worst troops are better than a lot of his best. That is why all of us are going. Makarov, there is an American officer joining you.

If he can't speak German, tell him to keep his mouth shut. We want nothing obvious to betray us to the enemy."

"Mr Hood, you and Mr Patton stay behind for a moment, if you please."

The rest of the command group gathered their notes and filed out leaving Hood and Patton behind.

"Lieutenant George Patton, sir!" the American said at attention and saluting. John nodded at him.

"We don't salute indoors or in the field, Lieutenant," John said. He looked over the man in front of him. He was not tall, his uniform was impeccable and he had a pie-shaped helmet under his left arm and an ivory-handled pistol in an open holster on his right hip. "Why are you here, Lieutenant?" he asked.

"Sir!" Patton said. "General Pershing felt observing a fully mechanized regiment in action would be beneficial, sir!"

"Were you with Pershing in Mexico?" John asked.

The Americans had finally become frustrated with Mexican raids across the border and had intervened.

"Sir, yes sir!" Patton said. "I had the pleasure of leading one of the raids, sir!"

"West Point, aren't you?" John said.

"Sir, yes sir!" Patton said.

"Lord save us all," John said. "A fellow collegian, Mr Hood. Major Hood is a product of Sandhurst, Mr Patton."

"Always a pleasure serving with fellow professionals, sir," Patton said, smiling. "You are a graduate of the Royal Military of Canada, sir?"

"Who me?" John said. "Thank God, no. I am but a poor farmer and part-time soldier, Mr Patton. You really don't know how hard it is to break you college boys of all those bad habits you have learned. Now, you have heard the briefing and seen the plan," he continued. "We are a light cavalry unit, despite what you have been told. Our primary function is to provide intelligence and support for the main regiments. In this instance, we will be employed to disrupt the enemy rear, much like your Bragg did in the Civil War. The only difference, Mr Patton, is that we are motorized. We are faster, more armored and carry more munitions than any horse cavalry possibly can. But make no mistake, we will operate much like the cavalry you are used to. Most of us are bilingual in German, so once we cross the lines, and even before, we will be talking in German. It will be night; the Germans have little motor transport and will not know we are not German. This will help us in our task. So if you can't speak German don't speak, and get rid of that stupid pie-plate of a helmet.

"Hood, you take Mr Patton with you, keep him out of trouble. And Patton? Pick up an Enfield before you leave. You are going to need it."

Two hours before time to begin John checked his field pack and weapons, making sure he had enough ammunition. He would be joining the initial attack on the small bridge, and wanted to make sure that all was in order. He waved Tatiana over to his side.

"Tat, you make sure you stick close to that radio man and you make sure that radio man sticks close to me," he ordered.

Like everyone else, she was loaded down with her rifle, spare ammunition, one round for the mortar and a Lewis gun spare drum. She also had the radioman's spare ammunition, as the radio he had strapped to his back was all the weight he could manage.

He could tell she was nervous, who wasn't, but she had control of herself. Quickly looking around he saw no one was near them or looking their way, and he reached out and tucked a stray lock of her hair back under her cap, allowing his hand to gently stroke her cheek as he pulled it away. She took hold of his hand with hers and kept it there.

"You'll be all right, Tat," John said. "We won't be right up front – besides, I am responsible for you, remember?

I won't let anything happen to you."

She grabbed the back of his head with her other hand and, pulling it down to her, she kissed him on the lips. "I'm counting on it," she said after some wolf whistles told them both they had not been unobserved.

"Whoa, whoa, whoa, cousin," Christine said. "I lend you my aide and ten minutes later you are trying to take advantage of her."

"Well you won't let me take advantage of you," John replied nonplused. "I have to take advantage of someone."

Tatiana gave him a quick peck on the cheek, then went back to her duty as the radioman's guardian.

"We are as ready as we will ever be, General," Christine said. "John, please don't hurt her. She has suffered enough heartbreak already in her life."

Then she spun on her heels and ordered the point company off into the darkness.

Two hours later they had secured the west side of the bridge and had extended a defensive perimeter around the approaches to it. It had all been stealth and knife work – years of training in silent attack were paying off now – and Christine led the first of the Eagles onto the bridge. All moving low and slow. Once they reached the halfway mark, the second company started onto the bridge, with the third and fourth making ready for an all-out support attack if it was required. Two mortars were set up and roughly aimed at the other side of the bridge.

"Once we are across, strip both those Maxims, dump them in one of our trucks when they get there along with all the ammo you can find. We might need them later," John ordered, then went back to watching and waiting for word from the east side of the bridge.

The third assault company was headed onto the bridge when the awaited signal was flashed back from the east side by signal lamp. The bridge was taken and secure. John jumped up and, with the rest of the troopers except for the hundred left to hold the west side, crossed over the Rhine and into the German homeland.

"So far we have not been discovered," Christine said when he got to her. "The perimeter is secured and we are manning the German positions to make it look like they still hold the bridge. No shots were fired and no one got away to give warning." The dark stain on the front of her uniform told that she had been more than just an observer in the taking of the bridge.

"Very well, Major," replied John. "Radio the go signal to the regiment, please."

False dawn was just breaking over the horizon to the

east when the horizon to the west brightened: the expected Allied barrage had begun on the German positions. If all went well, his first trucks should be crossing the bridge in fifteen minutes – and they were. Lights out, they crawled across the narrow bridge and the first twenty trucks fanned out to cover the approaches, then three armored cars sped off to the south to scout the way.

Half an hour later the lead scout vehicle reported the way was clear and that German military police officers were waiting to direct the 'reinforcements' to their assigned positions.

"That boy has balls," said the RSM, who would now be at John's side for the duration of the attack. "The Froggies showed up, about a thousand strong. They are going to secure the bridge after we leave."

"Good for them. All right, mount up – let's get the show on the road," John ordered as he climbed into his combat vehicle, all too conscious of Tatiana crammed up beside him.

"What did he mean about the German MPs leading the way?" Patton asked Hood.

"That's why we are speaking German, Lieutenant," Christine said. "The MPs think we are German troops coming to reinforce Cologne."

"You've got women serving with you?" Patton asked.

"More than a few," Hood said. "That one took out these positions on this side of the bridge, George."

They traveled up the road to Cologne at high speed, headlights on full, passing military police in German uniforms waving them through intersections until they reached their position overlooking the German defenses. The troopers took up firing positions all along the rear of the German lines, and the regiment's field artillery made ready to get into action. The sun was at their backs and they were keeping low, dust and mud covering uniforms and vehicles, so it was difficult for any observers to tell that they were not dressed in field grey, but in khaki. In any event, all eyes were on the Allied lines to the west, where the attack was expected to come from.

John looked back over his shoulder then at his watch. It was approaching nine am, time to start.

"Tell the Aussies we're starting," John said to his radio man, then, holding his flare gun in his right hand, fired a single red flare into the air. Seconds later, every field gun, machine gun and rifle the regiment had opened up on the exposed German positions before them.

The Germans reacted quickly, riflemen spinning around, returning fire, but machine gunners were not so lucky. Most of them were cut down in the process of trying to move the heavy weapons to fire at their attackers. The regiment's tactic of having one Lewis gun for every ten troopers paid off. As soon as a German counter-assault was spotted, it was cut down by the automatic weapons, and the now buttoned-up armored cars laid down massive fire from their Vickers and Lewis machine guns.

To make matters worse, the Australians, preceded by six tanks, launched a massive full assault across the bridge. Cut off from the retreat and attacked from both sides, German resistance slackened as more and more troops began to toss weapons over the tops of the trenches and hunker down on the bottom of them. Soon a large white flag was waving vigorously from the command trench and the firing on both sides stopped. In order to keep the Australians from firing on his positions, John had ordered that Canadian flags be flown from each of the one hundred armored cars and had hoisted the large battle flags on the top of his command vehicle. It was to his vehicle that the delegation of German officers with the white flag held in front approached.

The RSM flung open the hatch of the armored vehicle and, grabbing a Lewis gun from its mount, stepped outside followed by John and they met the Germans just in front of it.

"Well, cousin," said von Bekenbaum. "Once again you have done the impossible."

Reaching for the pistol at his side he pulled it out of the holster but, instead of handing it butt first to John, he leveled it and fired a shot. John, spotting what was going to happen, spun to his left and started to crouch while pulling his pistol from his holster with his right hand. The bullet from the Luger hit him and the breath was knocked out of him as he was blown sideways off his feet from the impact. Looking up from the ground, he saw Tatiana, feet shoulder width apart, her 1911 Colt held in both hands before her: she shot his cousin in the forehead before shifting and firing again, as the RSM opened up with the Lewis gun firing from the hip. Dropping the Lewis gun, the RSM grabbed John by both of his jacket's epaulets and dragged him to relative safety behind the armored car.

Tatiana pulled a knife from her boot top and, with a strength he did not know she had, cut away his jacket and shirt, exposing the wound, then spun him on his side to examine his back. She ripped off her own jacket and sliced it in half, jamming one half into the wound at his back and another in the front, trying to stop the bleeding. As John began to black out he thought he heard her saying in Russian over and over again.

"Lord, please don't take my love from me."

John woke to find he was lying on his left side in a real bed, in a real, warm room staring at a real, not canvas, wall. The only thing worse than the dry throat and mouth he had was the dull throb in his right rib cage and side. He tried to turn onto his back but as he did so a searing pain from his ribs almost caused him to pass out again.

"Aw shit!" he croaked.

Firm but gentle hands steadied him and he looked up into his aunt's eyes, his sister Marie, also a nurse, standing beside her.

"You've got two broken ribs and a hole in your side a truck could drive through," she said once she could see he was not going to pass out. "All of your parts are still there and nothing vital was damaged."

Then Tatiana was at his side, gently holding the back of his head and placing a straw between his lips so he could sip some water.

Nodding to indicate he was finished drinking, he tried to shift to get more comfortable.

"Sheeeittt!" he exclaimed.

"My dear," his aunt said to Tatiana. "You can tell how hurt a Bekenbaum is by the types of swear words they use. When they start taking the Lord's name in vain, things are not so bad."

"I love you too, Aunty," John said.

"I know, John, and I you," she said, kissing him on the forehead. "But not as much as this one does," she said, nodding at Tatiana.

Tatiana hit him on the shoulder. "You told me you would look out for me," she said. "How can you look out for me lying there? You told me, always look out for the unexpected. Yet there you are lying in that bed. You told me to keep close to you and I would be all right. Yet there you are lying in that bed!"

"And there you are all safe and sound, just as I said," John said laughing.

"Ach, men!" Tatiana said, stomping her foot and storming out of the room.

"And you can tell how much a Bekenbaum woman loves her man by how upset she gets when he does something stupid," Wilhelmina said.

"What are you talking about, Aunty? She is not a Bekenbaum," John said.

His aunt tapped him gently on the cheek and smiled at him, before she too walked out of the room, to be replaced by Susan.

"So the hero returns," she said sitting beside the bed. "It was close there for a while. Your RSM is waiting outside fretting, as is Christine. Stephan and Makarov have taken over the regiment; Makarov has been promoted to general and all kinds of important people have been coming by to check on your progress. If not for the quick action of that girlfriend of yours, you would be long dead by now."

"Please don't speak of Lieutenant Romanovchuk like that, Susan," John said quietly. "She is a decent and proper young lady who deserves more respect than that."

"Well, John," Susan said. "You better smell the roses and get out of that bed quick, before some other all-Canadian hero snaps her up on you. You kept calling her name while you were on the operating table and she hasn't left your side ever since you were let out."

"Oh, that's just some sense of responsibility she thinks she owes me," John said. "I wouldn't put to much into it. I don't have anything to offer a girl like that anyway, and now that I'm all crippled up … No, she is better off finding somebody else."

"That's what my father said about Willy and your brother about Ingrid," Susan said.

Then she stood up and waved to the door. The RSM, Alex Hood and Christine crept in. The RSM now had a major's insignia on his epaulets and Christine a colonel's.

"Oh Christ," John said. "See what happens when I am not around to keep things under control. They promote all kinds of incompetent fools without my permission."

John reached out his hand to shake the RSM's and pulled his cousin down so he could kiss her cheek.

"It's going to get confusing around home with all the Colonels Bekenbaum around," he said. "Nobody will know who anyone is talking about."

"Ya sure," said Christine laughing. "Just like all the Generals Bekenbaum running around."

"Now there is where you're wrong, Chris," John said. "When I get home it's back to poor farmer John."

"Oh stop it John," Christine said. "That shit might work on Tat, but we know better."

"I will have you know that I have never been anything but honest and honorable around Lieutenant Romanovchuk," John said.

"That is Captain Romanovchuk to you, farmer John," said Tatiana as she walked back into the room with a jug of water in one hand and a bowl of porridge in the other. "I have firsthand experience on how you tend to stretch the truth and your cousins and aunt have told me more."

"Ach, Jaysus," said John. "Can a man have no secrets

in this family? Major, you should run as fast as you can from these Valkyries: they will surely steal your soul."

Then he turned serious. "How are the troops?" he asked.

"Two hundred dead and one thousand, including you, wounded," Christine answered.

"Shit," John said. "In what, less than four hours?"

"They had five thousand dead and ten thousand wounded or missing," the major said. "That is more like the norm out here. Once again you looked out for us, General."

"Shit, all the parents and loved ones back home," John said softly. Then he sank back into the bed, fast asleep.

"That's why they all love you, brother,," Marie said kissing him on the forehead. "He cares more for them than he cares for himself. You better grab hold of him fast, Tat, before some French girl marries him."

"Oh, I have him already," Tatiana said. "He just hasn't admitted it yet."

The Armistice had gone into effect two days after their attack, and Currie had marched across the Cologne bridge and into the City eight minutes after that. The French and British took all the credit for that last push and the regiment did not care. They had come and done their jobs, now it was March and they were shipping off for home. To go back to their farms and jobs and the families that loved them.

 The regiment, John at their head had been paraded in front of the King and all the other Allied leaders, receiving their battle honors from the King himself, who personally tied the yellow ribbon with words Germany 1918 in gold lettering on one and Palestine 1917 on the other. He gave the proud ex-RSM his Victoria Cross for saving John's life, Christine the DSM for her actions at the small bridge and John the DSC for his planning and command of the action. The three also received awards from the French and Belgium leaders, and left the area clanking with all the metal on their chests.

 "It's too bad Tatiana could not have come to meet the king," John said as they entered their train coach, which would take them back to the regimental area in France. "She deserved to be there and receive her medal from him personally. I will have a cross word with my aunt when we return to base about that."

"Leave it be, John," said Christine. "Tat, for whatever reason, was adamant about not coming; Mom just went along with her wishes. I think it better that Currie award her medals in front of the regiment and the regiment alone anyway. Everyone but you considers her their adopted sister."

There was one final strange act before they left Europe for home. At the last moment and without warning, King George came to see them off personally. As Tatiana was still acting as his aide, she could not get out of meeting the king this time – he personally shook each trooper's hand as they boarded the ship.

As was his right as commander, John was the last to board, and he presented Tatiana to the king.

"Your Majesty, I would present Captain Tatiana Romanovchuk: she personally saved my life, sir," John said.

"Yes, I read about that captain: I was very impressed, and sad that you were unable to meet me in Cologne," the King said, extending his hand for her to shake.

She rose from her curtsy and said very quietly, "The honor is mine, Your Majesty."

The king looked sharply at her and was about to say something, when she put her finger to her lips.

"Let it be, cous— Your Majesty. For the love of God, please let it be!" she whispered.

The king composed himself, looked at John sternly and said, "As you wish, Captain Romanov, as you wish. John: you look after the captain. I have a special place for her in my heart after all she has endured and all she has done for Us and the Commonwealth." Then with a wave at the troops lining the railing, he was off.

Chapter Nine

And the regiment sailed back home to Canada. This time they landed at Halifax, to flags flying and banners waving. A band and pipers played as they walked down the gangway, formed up and marched to their waiting train.

John and Tatiana spent nearly every waking moment in each other's company, often holding hands and sitting, he with his arm around her shoulders and she leaning her head on his. They endured, as all those deeply in love do, the jibes and comments of their brothers and sisters, as that is what the regiment had become. A band of blood brothers and sisters.

All too soon for them, the trip was over and the train was slowing, approaching the Didsbury station, and everyone was primping their dress-blue uniforms, putting a final shine on gleaming boots and removing nonexistent specks of rust from spotless rifles or imagined piece of lint from shoulders.

The train stopped a half-mile short of the station as John had requested, and the troopers left the train and marshaled into their companies and lines. The colors were brought forth, uncased and unfurled and marched to the center of the regiment. John, Tatiana at his side, marched in front of the flags and came to attention. Without a word being spoken, four thousand pairs of boots thumped to the ground at attention and rifle butts slammed into the ground after performing the salute.

"It has been an honor to serve you, my brothers and sisters," John said in a voice loud enough that everyone in the regiment could hear. "You have done your king, country and regiment proud. You have upheld the traditions of our people and your families are justifiably proud of you."

John made to make an about-face when Tatiana bellowed out, "Three cheers for the general."

And in a roar that could be heard for miles around, the regiment belted out the three cheers, bringing tears to John's eyes.

"Regiment, attention!" he ordered. "Regiment prepare to parade! In columns of four, *regiment march!*"

John waited till the whole regiment was in line, marching down the road, before he began to sing in Russian the song the regiment had adopted as its own.

"*A Don Cossack was thinking of home,*" he sang, and the whole regiment picked up the song in perfect harmony, the beat matching the tramping of their feet. As they reached the town, all the spectators had joined in too, and the town echoed from the massed Russian voices singing their song.

John and the color party moved to the right of the formation, turned left and marched in place as the regiment passed them, until the center of the formation was in front of the colors, then with one last stomp the right feet came to the ground and the regiment spun, facing the colors for the last time. The song ending as they stomped to a halt.

"REGIMENT!" John shouted. "DISMISSED!"

With a final hug with their comrades, the troopers headed off to greet loved ones and friends left for so long. A pair of uniformed veterans took control of the colors, allowing the bearers to greet their families.

"Ya done good, John, ya done good," one of them said as they carted the colors back to the barracks, caressing the new yellow ribbons and fingering the newly patched bullet holes.

The Bekenbaums came together and as a group walked down the center of the road in two lines of three, in step, spurs and medals clanging as they walked. John was in the center, his aunt to his left, Tatiana to his right, Susan behind her stepmother, Marie behind John and Christine behind Tatiana.

Although everyone clapped and called out to them as they marched, no one got in their way or tried to stop them. They marched up the center of the street until they came to the large imposing sandstone house in the middle of the block, then, in line abreast, John keeping Tatiana beside him by holding her hand, they marched up the driveway and came to a halt in front of the porch.

Eight uniformed officers rose from their chairs on the porch and lined up at attention.

"General Bekenbaum reporting with a party of six, sir! One member killed, one member on extended detached duty, sir!" John said as he and his five saluted.

Andreas returned the salute smartly. "Very well, thank you, General. Now come give your mother a hug and introduce your old pop to this stunning young lady."

Members of the party sprinted up the stairs, the married ones embracing and kissing, the others hugging and shaking hands. All except Tatiana, who stood at the bottom of the porch, her hands behind her back and her head low.

Elizabeth slowly walked down the stairs and lifted Tatiana's chin to see she was crying; she folded her into her arms, stroking her hair.

"Welcome to my home, dear," she said. "John says such wonderful things about you in his letters. John, what have you done to this poor girl?" Elizabeth shouted over her shoulder. "You have made her cry, damn you."

"Oh no, ma'am," said Tatiana. "I was looking at your

family and I became sad. I miss mine so much."

"Yes, dear, we have all heard about it, and my heart goes out to you and the other girls, and to that poor little boy," Elizabeth said, feeling the girls trembling and sobbing against her breast.

"Does everyone know?" Tatiana asked.

"Only the close family, love," Elizabeth answered. "Not John, of course. Typical of a man, can't see his nose for his face."

"Please don't tell him," Tatiana begged.

"It would be better if he heard it from you, dear," Elizabeth said. "We have agreed that it should be left in the past and that you died with your family. You are welcome here as a member of *my* family."

"Liz, for God's sake, are you going to keep that poor girl out on the street forever?" Andreas asked, for which he received Elizabeth's tongue stuck out at him in return.

That made Tatiana laugh. "I think I will like it living here," she said and she bolted up the stairs to kiss John on the lips in front of everyone.

"So what do you think of the overweight and overdressed female now sir," Tatiana said lying naked in John's equally naked arms.

"You remember that, do you?" John said with a laugh. "It must have been the dress; it still makes you look overweight."

"Oh it's not the dress, John," she said. "I had to let it out so it would fit what was underneath it."

She jumped out of the bed and padded over to the pile of her clothing on the floor, holding up a large corset. She walked to the foot of the bed and began undoing a large number of buttons along the top of the corset.

"This corset holds what is left of my fortune and of my family," she said as she turned it upside down spilling the contents onto the bed. Diamond and jeweled necklaces, rings, bracelets and chokers spilled onto the bed in front of John's astonished eyes.

"Just as you withheld the knowledge of your wealth from me, so did I mine. And there is something else," she said, turning her head to stare at the floor for a moment. Then she raised her gaze and stood tall.

'My real name is Tatiana Romanov. I am Grand Duchess of Russia and daughter to Tsar Nicholas, last emperor of all Russia," she said regally and defiantly.

John said nothing, just sat in the bed looking at her. She withstood his scrutiny for a while then began to nervously tap her toes on the floor.

"Oh do that some more," John said, breaking his silence. "I like the way it makes your breasts bounce."

"You beast!" she yelled, throwing first the corset then herself at him, covering him with kisses.

"How long have you known?" she asked.

"I suspected something after the marquise met us for dinner that night. I had never seen her defer to anyone before," John said. "Then at the boat with the king it all came together. By then it was too late. I couldn't throw you back – I was hopelessly and madly in love with you."

"Oh thank you, John," she said burying her head in his arms. "Thank you for keeping my secret and thank you for taking me in and thank you for loving me and making me your wife."

"Tat," John said softly picking her up so she sat in front of him. "I don't care who you were or who your family was or was not. I only care that you have given me this and what is in this." He put his hand between her breasts and over her heart. "If I have that, I have everything."

She took his hand from her heart and put it on her breast and they spent the rest of the night proving to each other how much they loved one another.

A week later, they were riding back to the home ranch, each with a rifle on their back, a Stetson campaign hat on their heads and trailing a pack pony. John had taken her to the same beaver flats King George had visited so many years before.

"I can see how you love it out here so much," Tatiana said. "It is so calm, so peaceful. I don't even mind the mosquitos much any more. It is a lot like the Urals back home, though we were never allowed to go deep into them alone."

It was rare that she spoke of her old life and John kept silent.

"They would go through the motions, bring out the horses and letting us ride around the grounds for a while, and we could pretend we were Cossacks riding in the woods. We were never alone and never allowed to do or go anywhere even the most remotely dangerous.

"My father, oh how he hated your family, John, and oh how he loved you as well. You all have the traits he admired so much, but that he himself lacked. Do you know I saw you at a ball in Odessa? I think I fell in love with you then. You were tall and oh so handsome in that dashing blue uniform, and you danced with such ease and grace. The court gossips told of how you walked alone through the streets, as though you and not my father owned them. That not even the toughest of men would challenge you. Now I know why, but back then, I thought you some magical prince. Of course, when my father heard of my fantasies, he had a fit, forbidding me to talk or even to meet you. Oh, my father was such a fool John."

"You don't have to talk about all this, Tat," John said.

"Yes I do," she replied. "I need to set myself free of my past, so I may live in my future."

She told him of Rasputin and how her mother and sisters and she herself had worshipped him. How they thought he had a gift from God – how he was able to control their lives. It was not until she had spent time with Father Paul and with the regiment that she realized Rasputin had just been using them like everyone else to further himself. How her father insulated the family from everything that was going on around them. She had not known of the lives of misery and despair many of the common people lived. The rich land and business owners made sure her father was not informed, nor did her father really care about the common people. George had tried to tell him, but he would not listen. Instead of listening to people like Andreas, who told him the truth, he preferred to listen to those who told him what he wanted to hear.

Even her work at the hospital was controlled. She never left St Petersburg, and she only worked with high ranking officers, never common troopers. The girls were only ever allowed to attend closely monitored state functions and visitors were always approved beforehand and watched the whole time of their visit.

"I loved my parents, John," she said. "But they were out of touch with the people and with the times. My father trusted too much in his advisors, never doubting them. Still, there was no reason to kill him or the rest of my family. He had no more real power. Now all the people have is chaos. Father should have listened and modernized, like George did. He had just to look at how the Cossack bands operated for an example, or how the British constitutional monarchy worked. All the turmoil, destruction and death could have been avoided." She was silent for a few moments, then said shyly, "Just these last few months with you and your family, I have lived more, *experienced* more than I ever had in my life before I met you."

They rode along in silence for about a half an hour. Then suddenly she leaned over, grabbed his head and kissed him long and deep. "Now you answer some questions," she said. "Why do you keep saying you are but a poor farmer? Susan told me you paid for that entire trip in Russia, including your family, yourself. I would think that would mean you are hardly poor."

"Well, I was young and foolish and had a lot of money to burn then," John said. "Now I am older and wiser and have a wife to think about. You know wives: they spend a lot of money."

"I do not." Tatiana belted him on the arm for that.

"Well, I am a poor farmer, you know," John continued. "I tried raising horses like my father, but have no talent for it. Cows don't like me, so I have people who take care of them, and I don't know the first thing about crops. There: I am a poor farmer."

"But you have a thousand acres of land," protested Tatiana. "Good land that has many cattle and grows excellent crops, I hear. How can that be?"

"First, I do not own that land," John said. "The family company owns it and I am hired to manage it. I lease the land to others and charge them ten percent of their gross profit. I take ten percent of the calves every year and my, now our, cattle company, has cattle people who are hired to look out for and market them. Actually, I personally own very little. These horses too are owned by our cattle company, for instance. The house we live in is owned by the family's company and it is part of my compensation for managing the farm. I have a Model T that is mine – not the one we use, that is the company's. I own my clothes and the car, that's it. So yes, 'Poor Farmer' John."

"This is so different from what I am used to," Tatiana said. "Your whole family is incredibly wealthy, yet none of you flaunt it. In Russia, we would have a hundred servants and be driving a Rolls Royce, not a Model T. Our house would have a hundred bedrooms and there would be parties every month. You would be dressed in the best Paris could offer, not those work clothes you like so much."

"And every one would hate us, just like in Europe." John said. "Look Tat, if you want a Rolls or to wear diamonds and silk and live in a big house, I can do that for you. You know what I do with the money I get from the family business and the cattle company? More than a hundred children go to school because I pay for it. Thirty families never have to pay doctors' bills because I pay for them. I sponsor five of our brightest and best to go to university, whatever one they wish and can qualify for, every year. The rest of my family does the same or something similar. The family company funds the regiment totally, and the college in Olds and the hospital here and in Olds. Still we have more money than we need.

"The people see me working like they do. I pitch

bales of hay in July; I fix fences when I must; in the fall I round up cattle from the high ranges; and in spring I help brand calves. They know I don't have to. But tell me, Tat, how can I help my people if I am not among them? How can I determine what they need if they don't tell me?"

"Oh, my poor misguided family," Tatiana said after another ten minutes of silence. "They did everything you are doing but one. They never went among the people. Why do you think it was so easy for me to go over two hundred miles on my own? Nobody recognized me or knew who I was. It was so easy: be with the people."

"My father had to make it on his own," John said. "He had one lucky break – when your father made him a minor noble and an officer. But everything else? He has done on his own. I have grown up watching how hard he works, so I know. But our children would never have to work at all, let alone hard."

John went on to explain what he had seen in Europe, how the privileged classes set themselves up over those that had made and still were making them rich. How they had never experienced hardship or how hard it was to make a living. That it was their responsibility to ensure their workers and servants had enough to eat, put a roof over their heads and clothes on their backs, but that they didn't always meet it. The poor knew those lessons and helped each other when one of them needed it. Yet the privileged classes ignored the very people who made them wealthy.

"No," John said. "My children will be brought up as my father was. They will work as normal people work, attend school with normal people. Respect is earned, Tat, not purchased."

"Speaking of respect, Poor John," Tatiana said. "Can we not go home first before we meet your family? I need a bath and a change of clothing: I must smell dreadful."

"What we are going to do will not take long," John said. "It will not require looking pretty or smelling good. And a set of clothing has been sent over already and you can have a bath after, before supper."

"But what is it we are going to do?" she asked. "It would be nice if I knew what to expect."

"Just an old family tradition thing," John said. "Mother, Aunt Katia and Aunt Wilhelmina will tell you what is expected of you when we arrive. Which by the looks of it will be soon."

The trail they were following crested a hill, breaking into cleared land, and the sprawling ranch buildings were visible not more than a mile away. A large number of farm trucks, wagons and riding horses were in the yard, but strangely no people were about, but for some children playing in the yard. Not surprisingly, one of the older children spotted the two riders coming down the hill, and the whole gaggle ran into a large building, which the family generally used to hold dances and large meetings. John and Tatiana were met by two ranch hands, who relieved them of their horses, and John took the rifle from his back and placed it in the rack provided for them against the wall. Tatiana placed hers next to his as Andreas, Elizabeth and Katia walked out the door. John's mother and aunt spirited Tatiana away without letting her say a word, or saying a word to her, to a door that lead to a cloakroom.

"Good trip?" his father asked.

"Always is, Pop," John replied. "Everything good here?"

"Same as always," Andreas answered. "Weather was good, no wrecks to speak of. Stephan got home a couple of days ago."

"Will be good to see him again," said John. "Back to the same old, same old for me tomorrow, I suppose."

"Not for long," Andreas said. "Received some correspondence while you were away and Stephan brought more with him. You are about to become busy, my lazy son."

"Ach and I was just getting used to a life of

debauchery and drunkenness," John said, and both men had a low chuckle. A hand waving out of the cloakroom door signaled the women were ready, and John removed his hat, putting it on a peg, and followed his father inside.

Over a hundred people were inside: all the members of the extended Bekenbaum family – the youngest still at her mother's breast – were there, as were all the male members of Andreas's original inner circle. All had come dressed in day clothes, straight from fields, jobs or homes.

John and Andreas walked to the front of the seated assembly, talking to no one, then stood facing them. The inner door to the cloakroom opened and Tatiana, accompanied by Elizabeth, walked in and up the aisle to where the two men were waiting. Elizabeth and Andreas stepped back, leaving John and Tatiana standing alone in front of the assembly.

In German, John began to speak loudly and clearly. "I am John, son of Andreas, house of Bekenbaum," then he raised Tatiana's left hand with his right, his fingers intertwined with hers. "This is Tatiana: what is done to her and hers is done to me and mine." Then he gently turned her sideways and, taking her right hand in his left, placed both her hands on his chest above his heart. "So say I in front of God and man, in the name of the Father, the Son and the

Holy Ghost," he said, finishing by making the sign of the cross by kissing her on the forehead, then the right cheek, then the left. He finished by bringing both her hands to his lips and kissing them.

Tatiana took her right hand and intertwined it with John's left, lifting it above her head.

"I am Tatiana, daughter of Wilhelmina, daughter of Elizabeth; this is John, what is done to him and his is done to me and mine." Then taking John's hands and placing them above her heart and holding them there so hard his fingertips turned white: "So say I in front of God and man, in the name of the Father, the Son and the Holy Ghost," kissing his forehead and checks as he had done hers, followed by kissing his hands. Both of them looked deeply in each other's eyes, seeing the love that was there.

Elizabeth stepped forward and took Tatiana's right hand in her left. 'I am Elizabeth, Countess of Didsbury, house of Bekenbaum; this is my daughter Tatiana, what is done to her and hers is done to me and mine, so say I."

"So say all of us!" said all of the women in the crowd.

Then came Andreas, who had a large grin on his face. "I am Andreas, Earl of Didsbury, house of Bekenbaum; this is my daughter Tatiana, what is done to her and hers is done to me and mine, so say I!"

"So say all of us!" all the men in the crowd bellowed.

"Now give an old man a thrill and kiss me," Andreas said. At which Tatiana kissed his bald forehead, breaking up the whole crowd – and no one was laughing louder than Andreas himself.

One by one, all of the people in the room introduced themselves to Tatiana and then left to go to their suppers. Once again she was whisked away by the women, this time the whole group giggling like teenagers.

"Well I can see you can still walk, nephew," said Johannes. "You must not have worn it off then."

"Not for the lack of trying, uncle," John replied. "Believe me on that one."

"I had a hard time walking for few days," said Stephan. "Wow, what a week that was."

"Ach you youngsters," said Andreas. "Why I was out breaking horses the next day."

"Yes, brother, and a blizzard was blowing so hard you could hardly see your hand in front of your face as you walked five miles to the barn and back uphill all the way," Johannes said.

"Well, now that you bring it up brother," said Andreas. "Actually it was ten miles and I had to fight a hundred bloody Muslims both ways."

"Only a hundred?" John asked.

"Ya – the last time we heard that story it was two hundred," said Stephan. "Just like Uncle John and his three hundred bloodthirsty Cheyennes."

"I'll have you know it was four hundred, and Willy killed them all while I was fast asleep, all wore out," Johannes said.

The last was said as they walked into the family dining room.

"That is not true," Wilhelmina said as the men sat down at the table and began to pile food on their plates. "I only killed four: the other three hundred and ninety-six ran when they heard all the snoring coming from the tent. They thought some evil spirit was coming after them."

"Look at Mister Oh So Smug over there," Susan said, throwing a bun at John. "Did you hear what happened to Mr Big Hero over there when he was in Germany taking all the credit? When the big dummy forgot to duck, Tatiana held off a whole company of Huns *while she was stitching him up*, that's what."

"Yes," said Tatiana, "even after he called me overweight and overdressed, I saved him."

"You did what?" Elizabeth said. "No son of mine was raised like that!" Then she and all the other women threw their buns at John.

"Wait, wait," John cried as the women grabbed another bun each to throw at him. "I surrender – let me explain."

"This better be good," said Katia. "To call a woman fat and a poor dresser is a serious crime."

"Well it was like this," John began. "There I was, minding my own business, enjoying my cup of coffee—"

"Bottle of vodka, more the like," interrupted Susan.

"As I was saying," John restarted. "There I was minding my own business, enjoying my cup of coffee in Odessa, when I happened to notice that the very last refugee truck was unloading. The very last person off of the truck was a vision so bright, she blotted out the sun itself. Her golden hair shimmering and her sparkling blue eyes, setting off the beautiful silk gown she was wearing, only a hint of shapely ankle beneath the lace trim of her hem, above exquisitely tailored soft red leather dancing shoes. Never had Odessa seen such a beauty. Then the scoundrel commissar roughly pulled her aside to be his own. What could any red-blooded Canadian boy, far from home and loving family, do but save the poor damsel in distress. Outnumbered a hundred to one, I had to think fast or I and all my men would be gunned down and the lady left to a fate worse than death.

Thinking only of her safety and that of my men, I girded my loins and leaped into danger. 'Commissar,' I said, 'would Comrade Lenin and Comrade Stalin approve of you with such an overweight and overdressed Boyar?' 'But of course,' he said, 'you are correct, Comrade John: much better for her to go to the Imperialist Capitalists. Thank you for saving me from making a big mistake.' Truly, ladies, that is what happened."

"Well, you can certainly spin a good yarn," said Wilhelmina. "Much better than we have heard so far tonight. So Tat, what really happened?"

"I was not wearing a silk gown or dancing slippers," she said. "I *was* the last person off the last truck, and my dress was dark and simple, but well made. I was wearing a cap pulled down low over my eyes. The commissar saw the type of clothing I was wearing and the fact that I had no other possessions, and he pulled me aside so my hat was knocked off. He demanded my papers and of course I had none, and he was going to march me off to detention, when John came on the scene demanding to know what was going on. When the commissar told him to mind his own business or he would have him shot, John pulled out his pistol, cocked it, then pointed it at the man's head – and about a hundred Lewis guns cocked at the same time. 'She came in on one of my trucks, therefore she is my responsibility,' John said. 'Now if you want to die for the sake of an overweight and overdressed woman, who am I to say different?' The commissar backed off and here I am."

"Just as I told you, Lizbet," Andreas said. "John was always the sensitive one. Stephan and I would have shot the bugger."

"But, Poppa," John said. "I would have got blood and brains all over that pretty dress and what trouble would I have been in then?"

"Ah yes, my son," Andreas said nodding his head wisely. "Good decision. Ruining a woman's silk party dress is always a fatal mistake."

"It was not a silk party dress!" Tatiana protested. "It was a simple cotton dress! I wore it for my wedding gown."

"Oh, that dress," said Johannes. "I can see why you would be overdressed coming out of the back of a refugee truck looking like that."

This time Tatiana threw a bun, but at Johannes not John.

"Speaking of matches made in heaven," John said. "I hear you and our new Brit are becoming very chummy, Chris?"

"Very chummy?" Susan snorted. "Like mare-and-stallion chummy."

"Susan, be good. Tatiana is here," Katia said.

"Oh she is right, Aunty," said Tatiana. "I think if we left them alone they would be at it like two bunnies in no time."

Just like that, Tatiana became a true member of the Bekenbaum family.

After dinner the men were sitting on the porch smoking their cigars and drinking beer.

"John, I am afraid you are in a pickle," Stephan said. "That Arab Feisal is now king of a country called Saudi Arabia, and he wants you to go over there and build some refineries and pipelines for him."

"Yes I thought he might," John said. "So why am I in a pickle? That's no big deal."

"The Indian government wants you to go over *there* and build a truck factory for them: a fellow by the name of Singh contacted me about it," Stephan said.

"Again, why am I in a pickle?" John said. "I was expecting that as well."

"How can you be in two places at once, running two big projects at the same time?" Stephan asked.

"Like I run all my other concerns," John said. "Let a trusted partner handle it. Now, does the family business want to be involved or do I go it alone?"

"How much oil are we talking about?" Andreas asked.

"The Brits think it will be huge – the biggest they have ever seen," John said.

"Where is this Saudi Arabia?" Johannes asked.

"On the Arabian sea," John said.

"Are you thinking what I'm thinking, Johannes?" Andreas asked.

"Oil transfer station, holding tanks and specially built tanker ships?" Johannes asked.

"Didn't think about the ships," Andreas said. "OK, the family is in, but only with the transfer station, holding tanks and tanker ships. We give you your ten percent of gross for the contact, agreed?"

"Sounds good. What about the truck plant?" John asked.

"If you can get somebody to run it we're in; give me your estimates when you work them out. Fifty/fifty?" Andreas asked.

"On both ends, sure," John said. "Now, what about Europe, Stephan?"

"It's a mess," Stephan said. Quietly the ladies came and joined their men, sitting beside them, wanting to hear and take part in the thoughts and brainstorming.

"Well then," said Andreas after all the discussions were complete. "That pretty much brings us up to date. Next month we can narrow the discussion to things of immediate concern and updates on questions raised today. Now the time is late and this old man needs a drink and some sleep."

"John," said Elizabeth. "Your barracks room has been made up. No reason for you two to ride home in the dark."

"Thank you, my lady," Tatiana replied. "Sleeping in a real bed will be nice."

"No titles here, your royal highness," said Elizabeth. "I am Liz and you are Tat."

"Oh, Mother, always the joker," John said, turning bowing deeply to Tatiana. "Your royal highness the Grand Duchess Tat the Overdressed."

His mother cuffed him on the back of the head and Tatiana whacked him on the arm.

"Everyone here knows, John," his mother said. "But it had best be left with only us and forgotten as well. You are right. I apologize, Tatiana."

"Oh, I am more than a grand duchess, Liz," Tatiana said, sticking her nose extra high in the air and assuming a nasal English accent. "I am the Empress Tatiana and Poor

Farmer John is my Emperor." Then in front of everyone embraced John and gave a quick kiss.

"Ahem..," said Wilhelmina, laughing.

"Oh, sorry,," Tatiana said. "It is past time I get out of these smoke- and horse-smelling clothes and have a bath. Until then, my love." She pecked John on the lips, then flounced into the house, looking back at the door one last time, flicking her hair and hitching her hip, then was gone.

"Damn," said Andreas. "Do you teach each other that? My mother used to do that to my father."

"We'll never tell," said Elizabeth, as the rest of the women one by one mimicked the same motion as they went into the house.

"John can we talk for a while?" Tatiana asked later that night, both of them lying intertwined naked on the queen-sized bed that had replaced the single cot in his barracks room.

"Anything for my poor farm girl Tat," John said.

She was playing with the scar he had from the German wound as she thought how to say the next words. They usually spoke to each other in Russian when alone, but she wanted to do this in English and she wanted it said correctly.

"What happened after supper tonight on the porch, I

have never experienced before," she said. "All of you have an area of expertise and all of you ask for permission to do something, even your father."

"Yes, it has always been like that," John said. "Before my generation became old enough to take on responsibilities, they had a broader inner circle that had the same discussions."

"You allow women to have responsibilities and listen to their points of view as well, not just minor household items, real, important duties."

"Your minds are just as good as ours," John said. "Who do you think runs the farms and businesses when the men are away at war or on the yearly call to duty? There would be no food or business left if not. We have done this for centuries as well."

"I feel such a useless fool," Tatiana said. "Next to your mother, aunts and sisters, I have no skills, nothing to contribute. No useful education, nothing."

She was beginning to cry now.

"You are almost as skilled as many of our surgeons, Tat," John said gently, stroking her tears off her cheeks. "Your organizational skills running my headquarters were better than anyone's but my own. Your budget estimates were precise and almost always within tolerance."

"I don't much like the medical profession," she said. "I did it to be useful at first – it was the only thing my family would allow me to do. The other, well it is simple really. Not much more difficult than what I had to do at home for my servants and household budgets. My sisters didn't want to learn so I did it all."

"I need someone to run the new brewery and spirits division," John said. "Do you want to give that a try?"

"I know nothing about beer other than that I like the taste," she said.

"That's a good start," John said. "I knew nothing about wireless, other than that it was interesting, so I learned about it. I know little about truck building, but we needed to do it. The same with pipelines and refineries and pumping stations. I have people for that. You need to have enough knowledge to know what you want, then you find the best people to make that happen for you."

"Well, perhaps," she said.

"How this works is," John said. "The head of each division gets ten percent of gross profit of the division. The company will retain twenty percent. How the other seventy percent is distributed is up to the head of the division, but we like to see thirty percent retained for growth and unexpected cost overruns."

"And the ten percent would be my money to do what I want with?" she asked.

"Yes love, it will be all yours," John answered.

"Good, I need some new clothes," she said with finality and the deal was sealed, but not with a handshake.

At the normal Sunday morning breakfast, John announced the news to the rest of the family, who greeted it with enthusiasm, much to Tatiana's embarrassment.

"Nothing like sleeping with the boss to get to the top," said Susan, in her normal disregard for protocol. "What?" she asked after a series of groans came from everyone at the table. "You don't see Lionel complaining."

"I am, how you say? Learning the art of negotiation," Tatiana said. "Negotiation in business much the same as negotiation in war. Make subject careless, then exploit weakness. Make teary face then happy reward when get what one want. Nyet?"

"She's been hanging around you too much, John," said Stephan, laughing. "Learning all your tricks."

"Da," Tatiana agreed. "Ingrid help, give me good pointers. Also Mother Liz."

"Oh, Christ," said John. "I'm in for it now."

"Yes, my son," Andres said. "Lizbet is the best at those kind of negotiations. She pouts so delightfully, I just can't help myself."

"More like I'll cut you off for a month you randy old man," Elizabeth laughed.

After an hour or so of this good natured baiting of each other, the family broke up, each heading to their homes except John and Tatiana who returned to the barracks office.

"Ralf, you slacker," John said to his batman. "Get a hold of the RSM and ask him if he could meet me at one. Then see if you can find Major Hood and have him here at two."

After the fight in Germany, John had promoted Ralf to warrant officer from corporal for all the hard work he had done for him. Neither man would admit it, but they considered the other to be his best friend.

"Yes, your generalship, sir," said Ralf. "Right away, your generalship."

"Why don't you tell him how much you love him, John?" Tatiana said after Ralf had left.

"That's how we do it, my love," John answered.

"You Canadians, so hard to figure you out," she said. "When you are angry, you are very polite, when you are happy you sound angry. You treat your enemies and strangers with the utmost respect but with each other you are irreverent. You honor other people's and countries' accomplishments yet treat your own with indifference. John, your people are the most courageous and heroic, the most skillful and innovative people I have ever met. In Europe they would be making ballads and stories about you, in America you celebrated as heroes, yet for you it is nothing. Another day at the office."

"That is why no one takes us seriously or as a threat," John said. "It's not just us, the whole country is like that. The Americans have invaded us three times, each time thinking we were like the British and would fold quickly. Each time they were sent back licking their wounds, we are more like them than they know. Our country is vast and the climates are harsh, harsher than many places in Russia. It is spring now and mild. Summer comes hot and winter brutal. You are used to some of that; most Americans are not. We have to be self-reliant. We have few people and they are widely spread. If we waited for the government to help us, we would all die.

"Keep everyone comfortable with their superiority and what they think is our inferiority, don't brag, don't show off. It works, Tat – we own large pieces of American companies and they don't even know it."

"I will think of this," she said. "I am learning new things each day. I like how your family loves each other and is comfortable with each other. So different, so wonderful."

"Willhelm is here, John," Ralf said from the office door. He had picked up this was to be a friendly meeting not a military one.

"Wilhelm, so good to see you again," John said giving the man his hand.

"Same here, John," he replied. "Tatiana, still breaking my heart. Why you had to pick him I'll never know. There were much better men around."

"But none of them needed me like he did," she said, kissing the older man on both cheeks after hugging him.

"Been picking up the Bekenbaums' traits I see." Wilhelm laughed. "And what can I do for you, John?"

"You've been involved with the assembly plant since the beginning, correct?" John asked.

Whilhelm had been one of the original proponents of creating their own truck bodies to place on the Ford chassis and running gear. Now he managed the production schedules.

"Pretty much, why?"

"I need someone to go to India and set up a plant there; you interested?" John asked.

"Our plant or theirs?" Wilhelm asked.

"Joint venture," John answered.

"Payback terms, I assume? We supply the start up and receive the normal company percentage?"

"Ten years, thirty percent," John said. "Then ten percent every year after."

Wilhelm nodded. "Regular twenty percent for me?"

"Yes," John said.

"I have to discuss it with the missus, but I think it will be a go," he said. "She's never left Canada, so it will be a treat for her."

"Thank you, Willhelm, I appreciate it," John said shaking the man's hand.

"No, Mr Bekenbaum, thank you," Wilhelm said. "It's about time you realized how valuable I am."

"Get out of here you old bandit, before I change my mind," John said.

He pulled out a thick folder and spent the rest of the hour refreshing his acquaintance with its contents, while Tatiana looked over the Brewery proposal.

Precisely at two, Ralf knocked on the open door strode in and saluted. "Major Hood as ordered, sir," he said.

Alex marched into the room wearing his workday uniform, hat under left arm, and came to attention.

"Major Hood reporting as ordered, sir," Alex said as if reporting as a cadet to the schoolmaster.

"At ease, Major," John said, leaving him standing. "What exactly is it that we have you doing now, Major?" he asked, already knowing the answer.

"Sir, I am in charge of the new recruits, sir."

"Bloody waste," John said. "Do you know how to do anything else besides killing bloody Huns and training kids?"

"Not sure what you mean, sir," Alex replied uncomfortably. "I've been in the army since I was sixteen, sir."

"Yes, that is what this file tells me," John said. "This is the copy of your British Army file I was given when you were first assigned to me."

Alex had graduated at the head of his class at Royal Military Academy, Sandhurst. He had excellent mathematical skills, engineering and artillery skills: he was just the type of man John was looking for.

"Have a seat, Alex," he said. "Have you given any thought to what you might do after the army? The consensus is we will have peace for some time now, though not forever, and I don't think you want to spend the next twenty years being a wet nurse to runny-nosed kids."

"I hadn't really thought about it, sir," Alex said.

John outlined what he had planned for him if he wanted it. To plan, build and coordinate pipelines, pumping stations, refineries and oil-to-ship transfer stations in Saudi Arabia. Alex had already met King Feisal and the training he had received as an engineer would be an asset.

"What do you think?" John asked. "Are you up for it?"

"I don't know anything about oil or refineries," Alex said.

"Not to worry, we have people for that," John said. "I need someone I trust to meet with Feisal and negotiate a deal, then to stay on and manage it."

"I could probably handle the managing and planning part," Alex said. "But the negotiating? I don't think so."

"You will be going as my father's representative. Feisal was one of the lucky ones who got away from that Afghanistan battle my father fought. He greatly admires my father. You speak with Andreas's authority, your words are Andreas's words. Kings do not negotiate with kings. Kings go golfing or hunting or whatever it is that Arabian kings do. They have others to do the negotiating for them. Feisal has met me and you. He knows what we did for him and his country, and that we respected his people. So we will use that personal connection to hopefully work for us. Are you in?"

"Well it sounds good, sir, but…" Alex said.

"Oh: Christine," John said. "Take her with you. You will have to negotiate the terms of her employment yourself, as the managing director of the division, I am afraid. It might be wise if you married her first."

"But what –? How did you know?" Alex asked.

"You two have been undressing each other with your eyes since before we left France," Tatiana said, laughing.

"Ralf has a package of information for you on the Arabs," John said. "One from the Brits and one from Lawrence. Both are skewed to one side or the other, but you should be able to find a happy medium. I also include my copy of the Koran. I don't need you to convert, just understand it. They run most of their lives by it. He will also have a contract with our standard terms in it. They are for the most part non-negotiable. Read it over; if you agree, come see me tomorrow at home."

"Right, sir – thank you, sir," Alex said, standing.

"Ralf, get in here," John said.

"Your holiness, sir," Ralf said.

"Give Alex here that package I showed you, then get your sorry excuse for a butt back in here," John said.

"What's up, John?" Ralf asked once all that was done, plunking himself down in the seat Alex had vacated.

"I was always amazed at how well you did getting us good deals with the Arabs when we were over there," John said.

"Oh, it's a national sport for them, John. I noticed that

right off and learned the rules. Why?" Ralf asked.

"Want another go at it?" John asked.

"That oil deal in Saudi? Sure, what's in it for me?"

"One thousand dollars for each deal plus expenses," Tatiana broke in before John could say anything.

"What?" Ralph said. "I make more than that working for your husband's sorry ass. Ten percent of gross for each deal; ten years."

"You're insane. You want to bankrupt the company?" she replied. "One half of one percent, for one year."

"I could make more milking cows," he replied. "Five percent, fifteen years."

"You are lucky I don't have you horsewhipped for that insult," Tatiana said. "One percent, two years."

"My mother would roll over in her grave if I accepted such a deal," Ralph yelled back. "Two percent, twelve years, may my mother forgive me."

"Two percent, ten years," Tatiana said. "May my husband and father-in-law not horsewhip me for it."

"Two percent, each deal, ten years," Ralph said. "You will see me living in the streets in poverty, but fine, it's a deal."

"You impotent serf. My father-in-law will take it out of my hide, but yes, deal," said Tatiana holding out her hand.

They shook.

"She's good," Ralph said. "You should keep her."

Tatiana put out her left hand to her husband, palm up. "That will be five hundred dollars, please," she said.

"Five hundred dollars?" John asked.

"Yes, five hundred dollars an hour minimum charge for being your negotiating agent," she answered.

"Told you she was good," Ralf said, walking out the door.

"What do you need five hundred dollars for?" John asked.

"A new car and new clothes," she answered. "I don't trust that rickety old Model T of yours to get me to the doctors and the hospital when it is time, and I need new clothes to fit before and after the baby."

"Baby, what baby?" John asked.

"I knew you were a poor farmer, but even a poor farmer knows how calves are made," she said.

"We're going to have a *baby*?" John said, picking her up and swinging her around. "I'm going to be a poppa!"

Chapter Ten

It was a bright spring day in late May, 1922, and the sun was edging its way toward the still snowcapped peaks to the west at their backs. Unusual for the season, there was no wind that day and the smell of the new flowers his granddaughter had gathered for him filled his nostrils with their fragrance. Andreas had taken Stephan's two youngest on a quick afternoon ride and picnic and now they were less than a mile from home on their way back, following the small brook that would go by the ranch. It was the first time they had been allowed to ride their own horses, not doubling with other riders or being led by a halter shank, and they were still excited about being alone with Oppa for the afternoon. Andreas let his mind wander to other times and other places with happy times, as his grandchildren chatted excitedly over what they had done together that day. His brother Johannes had died of a stroke the winter before and Katia the summer after. One by one they were all reaching that time in their lives. Yet he and Liz soldiered on, as if time had stopped for them.

Their counsel was still sought after and opinions

valued, but more and more of the day-to-day running of things were being done by his two sons. How proud he was of them. So different from one another: one proud and ambitious; the other unassuming and successful. Both fathers themselves now, and bringing their families up in the traditions of their people. Never in their wildest dreams would Poppa and Momma have thought this would happen. How blessed he and his family were to have done so well.

"Oh, Oppa, look at the cute bear cubs," his granddaughter said excitedly, bringing Andreas back to the present.

On the opposite side of the stream were two grizzly bear cubs that had just spotted them and were looking to see if they were a threat. Spinning his head to cover all the points of the compass he spotted the mother. Shit, he thought, we're between her and the cubs.

"Children, do you remember what Oppa told you to do if we ran into a bear?"

Both children nodded their heads, instantly becoming serious.

"Now let's all be quiet and walk the horses fast toward home, shall we?" Andreas said.

The mother bear had spotted them and was still making up her mind if they were a threat or not. Then a series of events happened almost at once. Andreas's horse caught the bears' scent and was instantly agitated, then a ptarmigan picked that moment to break from cover right under the horse's nose, causing it to startle and spin away, stepping in a hole and breaking its leg with an audible snap. As it went down, it screamed in agony, startling the bear cubs, who bleated for their mother. She roared out her challenge and stood up on her back legs.

"Run! Run for home now!" Andreas yelled as he rolled out of the saddle and away from the now down and writhing horse.

The children kicked their horses into a gallop, letting them have their heads as the mother bear roared once more, coming down and charging the now-standing Andreas. Shit, picked a good day not to have a rifle, he thought, pulling his old .45 automatic from his shoulder holster and taking a sideways stance to the bear. He chambered a round, extended his right arm to the bear and squeezed the trigger.

Elizabeth and Tatiana were in the kitchen, and Tatiana was breastfeeding her second child, a daughter. John was sitting with Stephan, Ingrid and Wilhelmina on the porch, sipping a beer and bouncing his two-year-old son Nicholas on his knee. Tatiana had asked to name their son after not her father, but her little brother, and John agreed His second name, as was the family tradition, was the earl's name, and John had joked, "Nicholas Andreas Johnovich – Naj!" and that's what the family called him thereafter: Naj.

Hearing the horse scream and the bear bellow, John was on his feet handing the boy to Wilhelmina and reaching for his rifle propped against the wall, chambering a round and looking for a horse as the bear roared for a second time. Then came the first three measured and unmistakable Colt 1911 shots, followed by three more rapid-fire shots, then one more. One last shot rang as the two horses with the children clinging to their necks broke into the yard.

John swept a frightened child to the ground and vaulted into the saddle; gripping the horse hard with his knees, he spun it cruelly around and set it at a gallop back toward where the firing had come from, rifle on his hip. Stephan was right behind him on the other horse, Colt pistol in his hand.

As John rode away, ranch hands were dragging other horses out of the corral by halter shanks to be saddled when Elizabeth, her old Winchester in her hands, came flying out the kitchen door, skirts flying. Knocking a ranch hand away from the horse he was leading, she grabbed the halter shank and flung herself on the animal's bare back, taking off at a gallop after the boys, the Winchester held high in her free hand.

Tatiana came running out of the house; handing her newborn daughter to Ingrid, she and Wilhelmina sprinted to a nearby farm truck, which thankfully started right away. Tires spinning, they headed up the same path after the others.

John came onto the scene first, jumping off the horse and holding his rifle on the still bear lying in a pool of blood. He had not seen his father yet, concentrating as he was on the bear. Stephan came flying by his side and both men watched as the stricken animal breathed its last. They both heard the next horse come flying into the clearing and a rifle hit the ground as their mother screamed, "Ahndy!"

Then they looked around and saw him.

She had what was left of his head in her arms, putting his face and scalp back in place and trying vainly to stop the bleeding from his torn left shoulder.

"Ahndy, don't you dare die on me," she was crying into his ear. "Ahndy, if you leave me I will kill you."

"Ach, Liz," Andreas muttered. "How can you kill me when I'm already dead? Typical woman."

He saw Stephan and John standing behind her and smiled. "Women," he said, coughing some blood. "Can't live with 'em, can't live without 'em."

The truck screeched to a stop and Willy and Tatiana came running up. Both were experienced combat veterans and nurses, and both knew there was nothing that could be done. Tatiana put her arms around, John holding him tight.

Andreas reached into his pocket with his undamaged right hand and took out the flowers that were there, putting them one by one into Elizabeth's hair with great care.

"Your granddaughter was right: they do look good in your hair," he said, looking at his handiwork. "Just like the day we were married. You were so beautiful that day. I was the luckiest man in the world when you let me be your husband."

He brought his hand to her cheek and she caught it, kissed it and held it there while the light went out of his eyes, then she screamed out her sorrow to the sky, holding his broken and bloody body tight to her.

Thundering hoofs announced the arrival of four ranch hands and Stephan organized them while the two women gently pried Elizabeth away from Andreas. The six men placed Andreas's body in the back of the truck, John removing his shirt and placing it over his father's ruined face. Then he and Stephan helped his mother into the back of the truck, Stephan went to the driver's seat and John the passenger's, while Tatiana and Wilhelmina sat in the back, one on each side of Elizabeth, keeping her safe.

The truck slowly pulled away and back to the ranch yard. The yard was filled with concerned farmhands and their families, and as the truck came to a halt in front of the house the town doctor's car came roaring up in a cloud of dust, the doctor knowing from the looks of the women in the back of the truck that he would not be needed for the body they were guarding. He brought a blanket from the rear of the car, offering it to John who gratefully accepted it, placing it over his father's blood-soaked body to hide it from the children's and onlookers' eyes. A group of volunteers arrived with a stretcher and, after the women had escorted Elizabeth into the house, gently rolled Andreas onto it. At the direction of the doctor, they carried him into the banquet hall and placed him on one of the long tables there.

Susan came skidding into the hall, her hair all flying, rushing up to the table as the doctor was removing the blanket to examine Andreas. She sharply took in a deep breath as she saw how badly he had been injured. Looking around her, she shooed all the men away and assisted the doctor in his examination, after which she thanked him, asking if there was anything they could do for him. As the doctor left, Wilhelmina, Ingrid and Tatiana walked in the door carrying buckets of water and towels and the four women, softly crying, removed the torn and bloody clothing and began lovingly cleaning Andreas's body. When they were done, Tatiana sent the rest of them out of the room and, taking up needle and thread, began to sew up his torn flesh, starting with his shoulder.

"Thank you, father Andreas, for allowing me to be a member of your family," she said softly as she worked. "You were more of a father to me than my own ever was, and I will always be grateful for the kindness you gave to me. Thank you for bringing John into this world for me. You raised him to be a good man, an honest and fair man. Thank you for the love you showed him and me." Then she began to pray in Russian as her expert hands worked quickly to pull the torn flesh together, to make him whole again. As she was quietly working, the priest from town walked in and began to administer the last rights to Andreas. He had been trained by Andreas's older brother Paul taking over the colonies parish after he had died and, as he had been close to the family for years, the task was a hard one for him.

As Tatiana put the last dainty stitch on Andreas's face, Wilhelmina and Susan came in carrying his best dress uniform. Tatiana stood up and stretched, raising an eyebrow at them.

"Ingrid is with her," Susan said and the three women

began to dress the body as they had done with so many others during the war. Tatiana walked out to get her makeup kit from the car, and saw that the now dark ranch yard was filled with people, candles and lanterns in their hands. Some were kneeling and praying, others were just standing staring at the clear sky or with heads bowed. Many were crying.

Returning to the room, she saw, for the first time in her time with the family, Susan on her knees, her head lying on her uncle's chest. She was sobbing uncontrollably, her stepmother beside her, holding her shoulder. Tatiana knelt on her other side, placing her arm around the other shoulder, her head resting on top of Wilhelmina's hand and Wilhelmina's on her other shoulder. The three women stayed like that for a time, then Susan straightened up and the three took a deep breath each, looking in each other's eyes.

"Go to John," Wilhelmina said. "He will need you now. Susan will look after the children."

"Oh my God, the children!" Tatiana said. She had forgotten all about them the last few hours, her daughter must be starving.

"She is fine," said Susan, "Alice has her and has fed her." Alice was the wife of one of the ranch hands and had a one-year-old she was still feeding. "Go to John now." Susan took Tatiana by the hand and led her back out into the yard.

Taking up Tatiana's makeup kit, Wilhelmina began to gently cover up the blotches, bruises and stiches on Andreas's face, singing softly the German lullaby he and Elizabeth had taught her so many years before. Her voice was soon joined by others as blue-uniformed veteran nurses from the original regiment filed in, taking up their places around the body. When the lullaby and Wilhelmina were finished, their leader took her by the hand and raised her. "Get dressed now," the old major said. "We have him now."

    Wilhelmina took one last look at the man who had done so much for her during her life, who had meant so much to her, and walked slowly through the banquet hall door with a heavy heart. The veteran nurses as one did the sign of the cross, knelt and began to softly sing Russian psalms.

Tatiana looked frantically at the growing crowd all dressed in blue uniforms, looking for some sign of John, when a young sub lieutenant dressed in fatigues approached and saluted her.

    "Ma'am, would you follow me, please?" he asked. As he led her toward the radio shack he said, "We are getting worried about him, ma'am. The general will not listen to any of us, and he is frantically sending messages, not using any code, but in the clear."

They walked into the room and Tatiana saw her man, still in his bloodstained undershirt and trousers, seated before a radio, headphones on his head, rapidly beating out code on the key in front of him. Taking a breath she walked up and kissed him on the top of his head, putting her hand on his free arm as he finished the transmission.

He looked up and took the headphones off. "Only two more, Tat," he said. "Only two more."

"No, love, let these men do their job; your mother and brother need you," she said, gently pulling him to his feet and away from the table, putting her arm around him, edging him out the door and into the darkness behind the radio shack. She spun him around, hugging him; he at first resisted her, then his arms went around her and, burying his head in her neck, he began to sob out his grief as she stroked his hair in the clear starlit night.

When Tatiana stepped back and rubbed the tears from John's cheeks and kissed him, two veterans from the Boer campaign walked forward out of the darkness.

One of the two men handed John a Colt automatic, its action locked. "We found it lodged in the bear's mouth at the back of her throat; it's empty," he said, then the two turned around and wordlessly went to join their comrades in the yard.

John spent some time looking at the worn pistol, blood and pieces of bone still attached to it. "He went down like he lived, fighting to the end, never giving up," he said as he tucked the pistol in the back pocket of his trousers, The couple walked slowly arms about each other's waists to where the crowd of blue uniforms waited quietly. A delegation of ten came up to John and asked permission to speak.

"John, we want you to say the words to him for us," their leader said. "All the companies are in agreement."

John nodded his head, and he and Tatiana made their way through the crowd at the banquet hall and headed toward the house. As they were seen, the crowd turned and followed them, one man handing John the uncased regimental colors. Seeing that Stephan was sitting in the shadows of the porch, John stopped at the foot of the stairs and softly called out to him, while behind him the blue uniforms silently formed ranks. A dark figure rose from the chair beside Stephan and bent down, raising him to standing and smoothing his hair. She turned him toward the stairs, walking behind him as he approached the lamplight. It was their mother, still dressed in the bloodstained clothing she had been wearing when they returned. Stephan had changed into his dress uniform and was fastening the top button of the jacket collar when he stopped and looked out at the crowd. He looked down and saw a dirt- and bloodstained shirtless John below him, lying the regimental flag on the stairs in homage.

"Stephan Bekenbaum," John began. "The people have chosen me to tell you their wishes. The people wish for Stephan Bekenbaum, Second Earl of Didsbury, to lead them and guide them." Then he handed the regimental flag to his brother, who took it and kissed it.

"I, Stephan Bekenbaum, Second Earl of Didsbury, pledge that what is done to you is done to me, before God and man," Stephan said.

Then John knelt on one knee before his brother. "I John son of Andreas say that what is done to you and yours is done to me and mine; so say I."

"So say we all," the blue uniforms said.

Elizabeth, despite Stephan's protest, joined John at the foot of the stair, also kneeling and looking up at her eldest son. She placed her hand over her heart. "I, Elizabeth, say what is done to you and yours is done to me and mine; so say I."

Wilhelmina in her uniform was next, followed by Susan, and then everyone watched as Tatiana walked forward, her newborn baby in her arms and her two year old son holding her other hand. She like John had not had a chance to change yet and her dress like Elizabeth's was stained a deep red.

She stayed standing, her head high, but she spoke words so low only the family could hear. "I, Tatiana, daughter of Nicholas II, Tsar of all the Russias, Grand Duchess of Russia, pledge my allegiance and loyalty to Stephan, Second Earl of Didsbury," she said. Then she went to one knee before him, bowed her head and held her daughter above her.

"This is Andrea, daughter of Tatiana, daughter of Elizabeth," she said loudly. "What is done to her and hers is done to me and mine."

Stephan smiled and took the child from her hands, holding her to his chest and showing her to the crowd.

"This is Andrea, daughter of Tatiana, daughter of Elizabeth, granddaughter of Andreas; what is done to her and hers, is done to me and mine," he said, handing the child back to Tatiana.

"Come, Mother, brother, sisters, come to the house," Stephan said.

The women hustled Elizabeth upstairs to her room, while John walked over to the liquor cabinet and poured himself and Stephan a large glass of vodka each.

"Poppa," John said holding his glass high in the air, then downed it, copied by Stephan.

Stephan refilled the glasses and lifted his.

"Kaita", he said. Again both men shot the fiery liquid back and this time threw the glasses to smash against the wall.

The two men grabbed a bottle of beer each and sat at the family table. "Oh ya," John said, pulling his father's Colt from his pocket and placing it on the table in front of Stephan. "They found it lodged in the bear's mouth."

"Pop never ran from a fight," Stephan said. "And he never lost one that I know of."

"Nope, never did," John agreed. "That bear may have got him in the end, but he got her first."

"The first report I got was that he had hit her eight times, once through and through, out the back of her skull – that must have been the last shot. He stuck the pistol in her mouth and pulled the trigger," Stephan said.

"My God, but he loved Mom," John said. "Right to the end. I hope I keep that feeling for the rest of my life."

"When he put those flowers in her hair and rubbed the tears from her cheeks, my heart broke," Stephan said.

The men sat, staring at the empty pistol and holding full bottles of beer, thinking of past times, good and bad, with their father, neither talking nor moving.

The morning sun was coming in the kitchen windows when Wilhelmina walked in to see the two brothers, eyes still locked on the pistol before them. No one except the children had slept that night; they were all coming to grips with their grief. She walked up to the table and took the still-full bottles from limp fingers and poured the contents down the sink.

"John!" she said sharply, bringing both men back to the there and then. "Go to the downstairs washroom and clean up. Your uniform is waiting for you there. Stephan, your wife needs you to help dress the children: quick now!" she ordered.

"What about Momma?" Stephan asked.

"Liz is fine, better than you," Wilhelmina answered. "Susan and Tatiana are with her. Now go. Your family needs you."

One last, long terrible day, she thought, remembering Johannes and the day he died.

The family sat waiting at the table that held so many memories. Everyone except Naj was dressed in uniform, and even he was in dark blue. John had him on his knee and was holding Andrea in the crook of his right elbow. Everyone stood as first Tatiana then Susan entered the room, Tatiana coming and taking Andrea from John. Elizabeth entered. Unlike the rest, she was dressed in a white cotton dress. The cuffs and collar trims and the buttons down the front were red with gold and green flowers and leaves embroidered on them. Her silver hair was braided and the braids were wrapped around her head, with a crown of flowers woven between them. Even in her seventies, she was a stunning, trim, erect woman.

"This is how he first met me," she said. "This is how I shall bid him goodbye." Then she took Stephan's elbow and the family left the house and made their way through a parting sea of blue to the banquet hall and entered. At each corner of the table that held him, were two old guardsmen from the original regiment. Heads down, arms crossed on Winchester rifle butts, the barrels resting on the floor, they faced outward, backs to the man on the table.

Andreas had been placed on a stretcher made of woven pine branches, his old fur Cossack hat on his head, an eagle on one collar and a beaver on the other and a maple leaf in the center of the hat. Elizabeth came and gazed on his face. She looked back at Tatiana and Wilhelmina and mouthed *Thank you* to them, then bent down and kissed Andreas on the lips one last time, before stepping back.

Stephan was having a hard time, but his youngest son, who had been with Andreas, stepped up and addressed him.

"Oppa, we did as you said, and my sister and I arrived home safe," he said. "Thank you, Oppa."

All the adults in the room, including the guards, broke down in silent sorrow, they too remembering times when the man lying there had saved their lives.

Facing the inevitable and knowing Stephan was not going to be able to do it, John nodded at the eight men quietly standing against the wall, who came forward, four men to a side, and at a muted command hoisted the stretcher to their shoulders. The eight guards, three to each side and one in the front and rear, shouldered arms and, at the command, the door to the hall was opened and the stretcher party marched out into the daylight. Unordered, the assembled regiment, past and present, lined up in their companies and squadrons, came to attention and saluted as the body of the only commander they had known was paraded by them, the salutes held until the family passed them. The stretcher party was joined by the color party, battle flags were unfurled and a single saddled horse was led by Stephan's oldest son, Andreas's dress knee-length cavalry boots wedged backward in the stirrups . Not a word was said, not a drum or a bugle sounded. The family followed in two lines abreast, then the regiment in columns of sixteen, officers to the front of each company, and the only sound was that of boots marching in step.

Half a mile later, they came to the spot where a cord of wood had been stacked with care to the height of a tall man's shoulder. The pile was as wide as a broad man and as long as a tall man, and eight guns were lined up wheel to wheel, gunners beside their guns at attention and saluting as the party went by.

The bearers gently placed the stretcher in the center of the pyre and stepped back, saluting, then joined their troops. Then beginning with the eight remaining members of the original nine men who had joined him in Russia so many years before, in order of age, troop by troop, the regiments' members past and present marched up in line abreast, saluting the body on the pyre, then stepped back and rejoined their ranks. Every twenty seconds a gun fired its salute, until twenty-one had sounded. Then once the regiment was finished, the family in order of precedence saluted the pyre, ending with Stephan, Ingrid and their four children. Elizabeth did not, choosing instead to stand with her arm in the crook of John's elbow. The lone bugle sounded the Last Post, its haunting notes echoing off the hills and complete silence was held after the last note faded.

John looked over at Stephan and saw he was incapable of doing what needed to be done; he was barely containing his grief, hugging his oldest girls close. John released his mother's hand, patting it as he did so, and marched forward, coming to attention and saluting his father before about turning and facing the massed regiment.

"In the name of the Father, the Son and the Holy Ghost," he began, making the sign of the cross. "Holy Father, we ask you to place our father, mentor and friend at your side. He was a great man, an honorable man, to his friends and his enemies. He was father to us all, doing much for us, asking nothing in return other than we be true to ourselves. We ask that you help his grief-stricken family endure his loss, for the loss is great. Amen.

"Brothers and sisters, Andreas died as he lived, protecting his loved ones, sacrificing himself so others might live. Because of his actions and the actions of others like him, throughout our lives, he and we have saved countless lives, making the world a little bit better as we did so. Yes, a great man has gone, but he lives on in our hearts, in our minds and in the very homes and farms we all enjoy in peace. All this was because one man had a dream, a dream of freedom, a dream of hope for the future. Let the grief go: you know he would not like it. Instead celebrate his life and your lives each day you have left."

Letting that sink in for a moment, John picked up a torch and one of the old guard lit it for him. He looked over to Stephan, who was visibly crying now, then walked to each corner of the kerosene-impregnated logs on the pyre and lit them. Tossing the torch to the side once he was done, he rejoined his mother.

Elizabeth stood watching the flames rise until they reached the top of the pyre and then, tapping John's arm to get his attention, made ready to leave.

"Until we meet again, my love," she said, then turned and with John at her side walked away, until she passed the last line of troopers, then she stopped, turned sideways to look one last time at the fire, batted her eyelashes, blew him a kiss and, hitching her right hip, walked away. In her heart she heard him.

"Damn, do they teach each other that or are they born with it?"

She smiled and said, "I'll tell you soon, my love, I'll tell you soon."

Two weeks later Ingrid opened the drapes in Elizabeth's bedroom and turned to see her, lying in bed, eyes open and a smile on her face. She was dead.

Author's Notes

When World War I broke out in August of 1914, Canada, along with the rest of the British Empire, found itself at war. While there were many local militia units all across Canada at the time, these were mainly glorified men's clubs, just a chance for their members to play at being soldiers. The largest armed force in the country at that time was the paramilitary Royal Canadian Mounted Police, really a federal national police force.

The call to colors went out, and eastern Canadian British expats and their descendants flocked to the recruiting stations. Mostly non-British Western Canada was slower to respond.

One region of the Province of Alberta had been settled by a regiment of Prussian Hussars. They had received a land grant in Southern Alberta from the Kaiser as a reward for their service in the Franco–Prussian War of 1870. At the outbreak of World War I, therefore, they assembled a train and arranged for a large shipment of horses to be sent to Germany to help with the German war effort. This was of course not looked on with favor; the shipment was halted and confiscated and many of the people involved were interned for the duration of the war.

Letters received from Russian relatives and news reports of German atrocities in Belgium soon brought Western Canadians too flocking to the recruiting stations. The notion that the Canadian Expeditionary Force was comprised mainly of British ex-pats and their descendants, while possibly true of many Ontario regiments, is in the end mostly untrue. The population of Western Canada was and is mostly non-British in ethnicity, and it contributed significantly to the war effort.

As the war progressed, there was much anti-German sentiment in Canada. Even though many young Canadians with German last names were serving in the trenches and losing their lives, discrimination was rampant back home.

The war was extremely unpopular in Quebec, whose population, though French-speaking, did not consider themselves French, and thought of it as an "Anglo" war. Nevertheless, the Royal Twenty-Second, or Van Doos as we call them in Canada, a Quebec French battalion, made and still has a magnificent reputation.

At the beginning of the war, Canada was woefully unprepared. It had little equipment and an inexperienced officer corps. The British had been reluctant to provide a license to produce the Lee–Enfield rifle in Canada. In any case the Minister of Defense favored the Ross rifle instead, claiming it was the best rifle in the world. This was a Canadian-made sporting firearm, which of course had its manufacturing plant in the minister's home riding, and in which he had substantial share holdings. While a very good sporting and hunting rifle, it was particular in the type of ammunition it used and had a complicated bolt and firing mechanism. The RCMP had received a thousand of them to use and, after many complaints of failures, reverted to their old venerable Winchester Carbines. The most disturbing feature of the Ross was the fact that the bolt could be reassembled incorrectly after cleaning, which resulted in the rifle being able to fire without being locked, and shooting the bolt back out at the shooter. Many of the frontline soldiers would toss away the Ross and pick up an Enfield from the battlefield or as a replacement for 'equipment loss'.

 The British granted a manufacturing license to the American Springfield company, who started manufacturing Enfields, none too soon.

 As the war progressed, Canadian troops became renowned for their prowess and tenacity and, as they gained in experience, the Germans began to fear them. We were not a nation of shopkeepers. We were farmers, miners, lumberjacks, tradesmen. Most of us were used to the outdoors and primitive conditions. We were self-reliant and knew how to make the most of almost any conditions. Men developed a catwalk system at the bottom of trenches to keep their feet dry. They made railroads across the mud fields leading to the front lines, mining deep beneath the lines to create caverns to live in. German troops said the Canadians fired their rifles so fast it was like facing a troop of machine guns. We became the preferred assault or shock troops of the Allies, and the Germans adopted our tactics for their last offensives of the war.

    The Canadian medical corps became renowned; death rates were lower, and troops were back in the lines much sooner than the rest of the Allies' wounded. The Germans did, in fact, aerial bomb the Canadian hospital. It was thought at best that it would destroy the hospital and medical staff and at the least demoralize the Canadians. It did not destroy the medical staff. While lives were lost, it was not substantial. The hospital was up and running in a short time. Instead of demoralizing Canadian troops, it hardened their resolve.

    The Lord Strathcona Horse, a Canadian Cavalry Regiment, is credited with the last full-scale horse cavalry attack in of the war. They made a massed cavalry attack on a German trench system and, while they did prevail, it was at great cost in both men and horseflesh. Swords, lances and courage were and are no match for modern firepower.

A Canadian armored car unit was attached to Allied forces fighting in Palestine toward the end of the war. While it happened after hostilities ceased, this same unit was dispatched to Southern Russia to evacuate Russian nobility and did 'donate' their vehicles to the Soviets in charge of the district.

After the revolution, there were many rumors that the tsar's youngest daughter, Anastasia, had escaped, and a woman claiming to be her made the rounds of European society. (It should be noted that a Grand Duchess Anastasia did escape, but she was a cousin.) Grand Duchess Olga Alexandria, Anastasia's godmother, met the imposter in the 1920s and denounced her for what she was. DNA testing in the late twentieth century proved that all of the Russian Imperial family had been killed in the revolution.

Grand Duchess Olga Alexandria, along with her husband, children and grandchildren, immigrated to Ontario, Canada in 1948, dying in Toronto in 1960.

As mentioned in *Eagles Claw*, the Bears and Eagles had rejected the Ross rifle and were using German-made Mauser rifles. This move would have made them unpopular with the Minister of Defense and, along with their being of

German ancestry, would have resulted in them being left at home.

While there are a very few earls, or marquises in Canada, the titles in these books are just that: titles. There are no earldoms in Canada. I used the formation of the First Nation reserves set up under treaties as a basis for my fictional earldoms of Olds and Didsbury. In essence, the First Nation lands and people are a country within a country. While retaining their official First Nations status, they retain all of the privileges of that status. If they lose that status they become normal Canadian citizens.

For the reasons of continuity and storyline, I had the regiment conducting raids along a Turkish rail line on their way to reinforce and train Afghan troops. The Arabs, under the guidance of Major Lawrence, or Lawrence of Arabia, were in fact doing so at the time. I also moved up the time frame for the evacuation of the Russian nobility so the regiment could take part and still be able to contribute to the end of the war. Using the rumor that one of the tsar's daughters had escaped as a basis, I chose Tatiana as the survivor. At one point her brother and heir to the throne had become ill, and she along with Anastasia had stayed behind to nurse him back to health after the rest of the family had been moved to a more 'secure' location.

There were many German settlements in Southern Russia, or Ukraine, as it is now known. Some of them had been in place for over a hundred years. When the revolution broke out, many of them embraced it, as did the Cossack people. While many of the Cossack people favored the Whites, most of the Germans embraced the Soviets. Both groups suffered heavily at the hands of both sides during the revolution, and many left, joining relatives in Canada, leading to the largest population of Ukrainians outside Ukraine itself.

General Arthur Currie and the Canadian Corps did cross the Cologne bridge, but eight days after the armistice came into effect on November 11, 1918. There was no attack, nor were Germany's borders breached. However. Cologne was in fact under Canadian administration afterward.

British, American and Canadian troops did participate in the revolution on the Whites' side, mostly in Eastern Siberia, which is the closest part of Russia to North America. Distance, weather and primitive conditions doomed this expedition to failure.

During the war, Canada became the larder and factory of Britain, supplying much of the food and war material for the war effort. After the war, Australia, Canada, New Zealand and South Africa fought for and received more

German ancestry, would have resulted in them being left at home.

While there are a very few earls, or marquises in Canada, the titles in these books are just that: titles. There are no earldoms in Canada. I used the formation of the First Nation reserves set up under treaties as a basis for my fictional earldoms of Olds and Didsbury. In essence, the First Nation lands and people are a country within a country. While retaining their official First Nations status, they retain all of the privileges of that status. If they lose that status they become normal Canadian citizens.

For the reasons of continuity and storyline, I had the regiment conducting raids along a Turkish rail line on their way to reinforce and train Afghan troops. The Arabs, under the guidance of Major Lawrence, or Lawrence of Arabia, were in fact doing so at the time. I also moved up the time frame for the evacuation of the Russian nobility so the regiment could take part and still be able to contribute to the end of the war. Using the rumor that one of the tsar's daughters had escaped as a basis, I chose Tatiana as the survivor. At one point her brother and heir to the throne had become ill, and she along with Anastasia had stayed behind to nurse him back to health after the rest of the family had been moved to a more 'secure' location.

There were many German settlements in Southern Russia, or Ukraine, as it is now known. Some of them had been in place for over a hundred years. When the revolution broke out, many of them embraced it, as did the Cossack people. While many of the Cossack people favored the Whites, most of the Germans embraced the Soviets. Both groups suffered heavily at the hands of both sides during the revolution, and many left, joining relatives in Canada, leading to the largest population of Ukrainians outside Ukraine itself.

General Arthur Currie and the Canadian Corps did cross the Cologne bridge, but eight days after the armistice came into effect on November 11, 1918. There was no attack, nor were Germany's borders breached. However. Cologne was in fact under Canadian administration afterward.

British, American and Canadian troops did participate in the revolution on the Whites' side, mostly in Eastern Siberia, which is the closest part of Russia to North America. Distance, weather and primitive conditions doomed this expedition to failure.

During the war, Canada became the larder and factory of Britain, supplying much of the food and war material for the war effort. After the war, Australia, Canada, New Zealand and South Africa fought for and received more autonomy from British rule, and were no longer classed as British Colonies or Protectorates. A group of four prominent Canadian women led by an Albertan did in fact travel to Britain to petition the House of Lords, which resulted in women being classified as persons and citizens in the British Commonwealth of Nations.

Returning troops spoke of how they had been derided as "colonials" by the British populace and treated as inferiors. People of English ancestry in Canada tended to lord it over those with different backgrounds. As they were actually in the minority, this led to broadly held animosity toward the British and anything British. As Canada shared a border with America, the British reluctance to invest in anything Canadian, and American business jumping on opportunities to invest, led to greater cooperation with America. It's a relationship that is still strong today.

Much as our Quebecois brothers and sisters discovered in the early eighteenth century, the homelands we had left behind bore little resemblance to the lives we had created for ourselves in North America. The ruling classes in Europe had lost touch with us, and we had no intention of allowing their attitudes to resurface in our lives. One has to only look at Canada and Canadian people – how we come from many nations and cultures and how we have all prospered and made a great country – to wonder: what would the rest of the world be like if it emulated Canada's example?

Made in the USA
Charleston, SC
27 February 2016